# HER DARK CHRISTMAS

## A PSYCHOLOGICAL THRILLER

ADDISON MICHAEL

PAGES & PIE

Publishing ● Marketing ● Writing ● Consulting

2025 Pages & Pie Publishing



ISBN: 979-8-9927544-3-8

Library of Congress Catalogue-in-Publication Data

Michael, Addison

Her dark Christmas/Addison Michael

*Cover Design by Art by Karri*

*Editing by Tiffany Franklin, Bianca Salomon, and Jayne Shaw*



www.addisonmichael.com

*For my readers who think there should be a thriller for every season. Thanks for your loyalty*

# PROLOGUE
## ELLEN

**7 Days to Christmas**

If anyone had told me I was going to die today, I might have done things differently. Then again, maybe not. I've always tried to live my very best life, because I've learned from my brothers and sisters how short and fleeting life is. As someone from a family of children who were adopted out of traumatic situations, I know we aren't promised tomorrow.

My heart beats faster as the Uber driver gets closer to the quaint mountain cabin that has been my family getaway home for as long as I can remember. Nostalgia is my friend. I had a great childhood, and there are so many memories at this home. After all, everyone adopts fun versions of themselves on vacation.

My mind shifts through many favorite recollections but settles on the first time I was allowed to go out and play with my siblings. I'm quite a bit younger than they are, and Mom was always so protective of me. She made my older brother, Thad, promise not to play rough, when really, it was always my sisters, Kelsey and Casey, who liked to stir things up. I smile as I reminiscence.

We played for hours that day. It started with snowmen. We each built one in our own likeness. Mine was my exact height. I had used my hat and scarf, despite the cold. It was worth it to win the challenge. Then we had a snowball fight, ducking behind the snowmen, deeming them *protecting ice men*. But it wasn't until we built a snow fort that everything changed. I was the only one small enough to tunnel through to the other side. When I accomplished the goal, my older sisters cheered for me like I was the hero of the day. Thad attempted to lift me onto his shoulders, but we both ended up falling in the snow. We had so much fun that we made those three events holiday traditions. I smile with a sudden thought. Maybe I'll suggest we do an adult version this week.

The sun hasn't even risen in the sky. It was an early flight, and I'm tired, but excitement pulses through me, and I cover my mouth so I don't giggle out loud. I told Mom I'd arrive later this morning so I can surprise her. I glance at the seat next to me, eyeing my gifts for the family. There are so many, I couldn't fit them in the trunk.

Okay, maybe I went overboard. But I love Christmas, and I love my family. What better way to show them how much than to give them these amazing gifts? Some are silly, like the vintage Kriss Kross CD I found for my sister and the plastic tube of hair gel that's the exact brand my brother used to cake on his hair when we were growing up. But I put a lot of thought into the cashmere throw blanket for Mom. I hope it brings her relaxation as time continues to age her. Admittedly, this is my first year as a social worker, so I might have overspent. It's not exactly a lucrative career, but once I obtained my last certification, they promoted me into management, and that came with a nice pay bump.

As we get closer to the cabin, I contemplate how I will get my luggage and all these gifts into the house. The Uber comes to a stop. I pay the driver through the app and hop out of the car. He pops the trunk and pulls out my suitcase. I thank him and shut the trunk. I look up expecting to see my favorite view of the crisp mountains with white-capped peaks as the sun begins to rise.

A nervous squeak pops out. A person is standing by the car. I'm not normally jumpy and I laugh when I see who it is. My favorite sibling, Blinker. Blinker could not be more different than me. Not just physically, but personality-wise. Where I'm laid back, Blinker is intense and focused. Maybe that's why I connected to this sibling. We aren't related by blood, so nothing is hereditary, but I always wished I was stronger and more independent like Blinker. There's a huge age difference between me and my siblings, and I don't have the best memories with all of them. But Blinker was always kind to me. The person who didn't pat me on the head in a condescending *little sister* way. But something feels off right now. Blinker stares at me with hard eyes.

"Hey!" I throw my arms around Blinker. My heart does a little double skip with anxiety as I remember the last conversation we had. Out of nowhere, Blinker said some really mean things to me. Even now, this embrace feels a little cold and distant. I try not to shudder. Still, I'm determined to put that behind me. Maybe all the repressed feelings came out during that tirade, and we can move on now.

I lift my chin in determination and step back. "Can you help me get these presents?"

"Of course." Blinker smiles now, and I feel all apprehension dissolve. That face, so full of character, lightens in this moment. Reaching into the back seat and grabbing as many presents as possible, Blinker turns to me. "You know, we should put these in the woodshed for now so they will be a huge surprise on Christmas morning."

"Oh!" I think about this for a minute. "I really was just going to put them inside under the tree... Do you think the woodshed is clean enough?" I always try to get along with everyone and be as little trouble as possible, and right now is no exception. If Blinker thinks we should, I'll check it out.

Blinker nods.

"Okay." I reach into the car and grab the rest of the presents. With everything loaded in our arms, I nod at the Uber driver and watch him drive off.

"Leave the suitcase for now, we can get it in a minute," Blinker calls.

I agree and turn to follow Blinker into the woodshed. It *will* be more fun to surprise my family with presents showing up under the tree on Christmas morning.

Hands full, I turn to find Blinker already standing with the door open to the woodshed, waiting for me with empty arms. *That was fast.* The gifts must have been heavy. I make my way over and take a step into the old building, which is more of a storage space. I view it critically. I really don't want to ruin the prettily wrapped presents in my arms.

I'm hit with the smell of turpentine, and dust tickles my nose. As my eyes adjust to the compact area, I see a large spider web in the corner with a spider climbing on it. I see old storage boxes stacked precariously under it. They look like they're rotting, and there are water stains on some of them. There's a snowmobile with a canvas cover in the middle, taking up most of the space. I know it hasn't worked for years.

"Blinker, I don't think—" But my words are cut off when I take a step back, bumping into the solid person who is once again staring wordlessly at me. Blinker reaches backward and slams the door shut. I'm so startled I drop my packages. "Shoot!"

There's a strange look in Blinker's eye that holds me frozen in place. I can see the darkened pupils, and I know they dilate in the dark to let in more light, but this is different. I can feel the energy coming off Blinker shift. Blinker is putting off a dangerous vibe.

Murderous.

I'm not entirely surprised when Blinker is behind me in a sudden move, circling an arm around my shoulders, and something sharp presses against my throat. I gasp as the cold object pushes hard against my larynx, cutting off my ability to speak.

"People like you make me sick," Blinker hisses in my ear. "You stole my life."

"Wha—" I try to croak out a response, but I can't speak. It hurts too bad. The object is sharp and stunningly painful. I try to understand what these words mean. I've never stolen anything. I was way younger than all my siblings, but we were still close. When teenage girls at school were mean to me, Blinker would assure me they were just jealous and not worth my energy. I can't imagine what would trigger Blinker to say such a thing.

I am having a hard time breathing now, and it feels like my neck is slick with sweat. Then the pain gives way to shock, and my brain starts to slow down. I'm having a hard time forming thoughts. But I don't think it's sweat on my neck. With a start, I realize it must be blood. Lots and lots of blood coating my neck.

I'm falling now. I hit the ground hard, and I lay there, welcoming the numbness that is spreading through my limbs. It feels better than agony. I am starting to feel weightless, like my soul is detaching from my body.

As my mind blissfully embraces the darkness, I feel peace flood through me. I wish only good things for Blinker's life. The person I always thought understood me. Suddenly, it feels so important to say something profound. Unconditional. No matter what Blinker has done to me, no matter why, I croak the words, and I can only hope they are clear.

"I love you."

# GLASGOW COMMUNITY TIMES

MARCH 13, 2006

## SPELLING PRODIGIES

Ten-year-old twin sisters, Kelsey and Casey Caper, will represent Glasgow Middle School at districts in our annual Northeastern Montana Spelling Cats Spell Off. It's rare to have two kids from the same family represent our school in a spelling bee. Rarer still is it to have twin sisters who spell competitively. They say there's a psychic link between twins, and these sisters are no exception. Marney Caper, the girls' mother, had this to say about her daughters: "I could not be prouder of the way Kelsey and Casey always encourage each other to be better and find talents they didn't realize they had. We will be in the audience cheering on both girls equally. Go, Spelling Cats!"

# ONE

KELSEY

**14 Days to Christmas**

"Come on, Kels, you have to come!" Casey's voice is excited, if a bit pushy. She's been busy working full-time and living with her boyfriend, Brax, while I've been busy pursuing my degree. In short, we've lost touch. Sure, there are occasional, quick phone calls and texts. But these days, Casey lives her life tattooing her clientele, and I live mine, which, until a week ago, consisted of attending college and writing my dissertation. It doesn't feel real that I have a PhD now. It was a lot of hard work, and I'm trying to figure out what is next.

"Why? Give me a good reason why I should go." My new degree, mixed with good old-fashioned logic, is telling me a family holiday getaway is a very bad idea. I take a sip of the coffee I just made myself and find it's too hot. It burns my mouth, and I jerk the cup away, dribbling the scalding brown liquid down my red fleece sweater. I shake my head with resignation. Today must be a clumsy day.

I'm lucky I can wear red. Lots of people tell me that not all blonds with blue eyes can pull it off. I'm also one of the lucky light-haired women who is not required to wear makeup. At least I have that going for me.

"The eights," Casey says as if it's the most obvious explanation there is. She acts like I should know exactly what she's talking about.

I dab the spot from my sweater with a dishcloth and rack my brain for the significance of *the eights*. As I rest a hip against my kitchen counter and blow on my coffee, I say, "Please do not use numerology to try to convince me to buy an expensive plane ticket to stay in the mountains in *Middle-of-Nowhere*, Montana, with a barely functioning family when I need to be looking for a job."

"Barely functioning?" Casey snorts. "I take offense at that. And it's not only about numbers. It's more about fate and the universe telling you where to go. Eight of us together on December eighteenth, eight days before Christmas. Eight, eight, eight," Casey sums up.

At my silence, Casey lets out a loud huff as if I'm making her do a lot of work. She continues her explanation. "The number eight represents finding balance and new beginnings."

I have to admit I am intrigued, but Casey is not very detail-oriented. It's actually seven days to Christmas. I don't point that out. Instead, I ask, "New beginnings?"

Now, it's Casey's turn to go silent.

I wait her out. I took a whole class on allowing the

patient to speak first. (Well, that's not all we learned, but I did learn the power of silence.)

"You can't deny that we've all drifted apart. When you left to go to college, you never came back. Not even on holidays or special occasions."

It's true. I never felt more peace than the day I moved out. I love them all. I do. But, like every other family, we have our share of dysfunction, and I was so tired of the drama. The more I studied, the more I found our dynamics were similar to many others. Everyone has dysfunction. It's just a matter of to what degree we respond to it.

"I mean, I get it, sort of. You picked a really hard major, and you wanted to go live your life. We just missed you is all." Casey talks faster when she gets anxious. She must be worried her words will set me off. Lucky for her, I've grown a lot in college. I'm not that quick-tempered, blunt, self-centered teenager anymore. I decide to let her off the hook.

I chuckle. "I know we've drifted apart, Case. I just see that differently. Mom and Dad raised us to go into the world and live our lives independently. That's what we've been doing. It's healthy."

"Ugh." She groans, her tone growing increasingly emphatic as she speaks. "You sound just like a therapist. How are we the same age? You're so much more mature than me!"

I hear a buzzing noise, and I pause a minute. Is she tattooing while she's on the phone? I shouldn't be surprised. Casey has always been a bit chaotic.

"I'm older than you." I take a sip of my coffee, which is now just right. I take it to the couch and sit, pulling my feet up beside me.

"*Really*? By five months. Way to get us off topic, by the

way. Are you packing your bags right now or not?" Casey pushes.

"Not," I decide. "Your math isn't working here. It's December eighteenth, not the eighth, and how are there going to be eight people? There are four of us—you, me, Ellen, and Thad—plus Mom and Dad. That's six."

"I'm bringing Brax, and Thad is bringing Melly," Casey explains.

"Oh, right. I really like Melly." The words pop out of my mouth before I realize the implications of what I'm not saying. I flinch. So much for that new self-control I've been practicing.

"Thanks a lot, asshole!" Casey snipes.

"Calm down. I like Brax too. He's just not as good at girl talk."

Casey laughs.

That was a good save. It's not that I don't like my sister's boyfriend. He's fine. I don't have much of an opinion at all, really. Though sometimes I wonder if he's good enough for her. I don't mean that in a judgmental way. It's just my job as the oldest to think about things like how he treats Casey. Not to mention, I did some digging into his background. It's not my business, but it was part of an assignment. Brax has a record. I wonder if Casey knows that.

Casey was adopted when she was seven. From that point until I moved away to college, we were inseparable. She's my age and easily slipped into the role of my lost twin sister. In fact, we told people we were fraternal twins. We couldn't pull off *identical* on account of Casey's rich brown hair and deep brown eyes. That and the fact that Casey was different from me in every way. She was tall and athletic, where I'm petite. I chose color guard in high school, while Casey ran track.

Still. We thought we had everyone convinced we were twins. Especially since it's an unspoken rule in our family not to tell people we are adopted. Mom and Dad thought that would break down the family bond. Knowing what I know now, I disagree. There were a lot of things Mom and Dad did that I would have done differently. Hence the dysfunctional childhood.

"Give me another reason I should go," I push.

"I'll be there. How can you say *no* to that?" Casey smarts.

"Easy. Like this. *No*."

If only I had stuck to my boundaries.

# HELENA HERALD

JULY 1, 2001

## SIMMONS FAMILY SLAUGHTER

The bodies of Jan and Michael Simmons were found brutally murdered in their home just after midnight. Police responded to a 911 crisis call from Mrs. Simmons prior to her death. Police caught and arrested a 37-year-old man. The suspect is being held without bail. "Obviously, we're devastated by this loss. It's a sad night in Helena, Montana. But we are happy we were able to rescue one of the family members. Our hearts go out to Kelsey Simmons—the lone survivor," said Police Chief Solsbeck.

# TWO

KELSEY

**14 Days to Christmas**

"It was just a dream," I tell myself over and over, but it's not true. Tonight, it was a dream, but once upon a time, it was all real. I'm a psychologist. Correction, I just got my PhD. I haven't accepted a position yet, but I'll be the first one to say that lately, my repressed memories are fighting like mad to resurface. In an extreme effort to function, I push them back down. Just like I always do. I know this isn't healthy.

Awareness is one thing. Healing is another. It's a process filled with intense bursts of pain. There's no short-cut. I'll have to sit with my feelings, but I'm not in a place where I can go through it. I'm not ready. I don't know if I'll ever be ready.

I actively ignore the night when I was five years old and woke to a piercing scream coming from the bed next to me where my twin sister, Kammy, had been sleeping. That scream cut off abruptly when a man slit her throat. Right in front of me. Peeking out from underneath my comforter, my mind barely registered the trauma when the man turned his attention to me. My body quaked inwardly while I lay there paralyzed in fear.

As he threw back the comforter, I smelled a familiar scent of deodorant, but I never saw his face. I felt his warm hand on my shoulder. A cold, wet steel blade pressed against my neck, then the pressure stopped. Suddenly, there was a pandemonium of shouting. But I heard only one voice that boomed in the dark. The voice of a savior.

"Freeze!"

Someone flipped on the lights, and it was almost worse than the shadowy chaos. It flooded into my retinas, temporarily blinding me. I blinked furiously as my eyes adjusted to the sight in front of me. Police were handcuffing the man who was about to kill me. I had a sense that there were many people crammed into the small room. Chaos hung in the air. But all I saw was blood. It was everywhere, running onto my sister's white bedsheets.

I rushed to her side. Her eyes were closed, and I knew she was dead. That bond, our twin link, had been severed, along with her neck, leaving me feeling cold and lifeless. I'll never forget that void of nothing, like she had abandoned me, casting me into a life of solitude.

I put my hands on her neck to stop the bleeding or perhaps just to cover it up. I wanted to scoop the blood off the mattress and put it back into her body so her eyes would flutter open, like when she woke up first thing in the morning. When that didn't work, I wanted to stop seeing the blood, so I took my sister's blanket and gently placed it over the pooling, spilling blood. Someone shook my shoulder. It was a police officer.

"Please." I leaned down and whispered to my sister. "Don't leave me."

A loud wail sounded in the room, and as I looked up at the officers swarming, I was startled to find it was me. I was making that awful sound. I wanted to chase down the man they were taking out of the house and loading into the police car to ask him *why*. Why would someone take my twin sister from me like this?

It was less than an hour later when I discovered that he had taken my mom and dad from me too, brutally murdering them all. In one night, my whole family was stolen from me. I was the lone survivor of the Simmons Family Slaughter.

# WARNING

WINTER WEATHER ADVISORY

The National Weather Service Billings, Montana
6:30 PM MST WED December 18, 2025

Potentially dangerous winter weather is expected within
the next 12 to 36 hours or is occurring. Travel difficulties
expected.

# THREE

KELSEY

**7 Days to Christmas**

I scroll through my phone as I stand in line to get a coffee before I catch my plane to Billings, Montana. There's a winter weather advisory in effect tonight, and it looks like we can expect ten inches of snow and gusts of wind up to fifty miles per hour. My plane is set to land well in advance of that time. From Billings, I'll hire an Uber to take me up the Bighorn Mountains to my family's large, roomy cabin, where we will all likely get snowed in for the week leading up to Christmas.

"I'll Be Home for Christmas" plays over speakers throughout the airport, and I can see about five decorated Christmas trees situated outside restaurants and shops that add to the ambiance. Twinkle lights wrap the flight information display system. I snort to myself. As if the decorations and the uninspired gift cards in the front zipper of my carry-on would ever let me forget it is Christmas time.

But what goes through my head as I wheel my carry-on behind me, shifting forward in the coffee line and absently twirling my phone with one hand is, *Why am I not using the winter weather advisory as an excuse to cancel this trip?* Lord knows I didn't want to go in the first place. Then I remember. Once I make up my mind and plan things out, it feels impossible to back out. I want to see them through.

I was solid on my conviction to not attend this family holiday until I made an appointment with my therapist, who challenged me to meditate and journal about it. Once I worked through my feelings, I realized we are all adults now, and it's not healthy to hold childish resentments toward my adult siblings. I decided I should go. Not to mention, once Casey talked me into it, I gave her my word.

My hesitation was due to the last memory I had in that cabin—not a good one. It was a summer vacation. We were all teenagers taking our hormones and anger out on each other the whole trip. I had a hard time forgiving Casey for calling me a *Controllo*, poking at my need to always be in charge.

More than once, Mom sent us all to our rooms like she did when we were kids. I have to say, while I enjoyed the silence and temporary reprieve from the fighting, I hated the feeling that I was in trouble. I was always the good kid, the overachiever, the kid who told everyone at school that my family was the best thing that ever happened to me and that we adored each other.

I look back now, and I feel grateful that I was adopted into this family. But my words when I was growing up were lies. I just really wanted people to think we were normal and perfect. But we were so far from that.

"Miss, the line is moving." The person behind me pokes my shoulder, then points to the gap.

I shake my head at my daydreaming and move forward, my brain sticking on the word *perfect*, which makes me shudder. There's no such thing, and my constant need to try to attain perfection nearly crippled me at one point in my degree program. I was so afraid to fail, I landed in the hospital with an irregular heartbeat. I had slept only a few hours a night the week leading up finals and had eaten very little. When I ran out of time and left several answers blank on an exam, I collapsed. Thankfully, they diagnosed it as a panic attack—much to my embarrassment—and once I knew what signs to look for, I figured out what to do when I felt one coming on. More importantly, what I need to do to avoid them.

As I order my coffee and stand to the side to wait for them to call my name, I watch the baristas move around, quickly making drinks. I gauge how many people are in line before me. My heart rate picks up. I pull on the collar of my black sweatshirt because suddenly, it feels tight around my neck. I feel a trickle of sweat drop down the length of my spine. The phone in my hand is shaking as I press my thumb against the screen.

I text my therapist. Yes, I have a therapist who allows me to text her when I struggle.

Kelsey: *I don't feel so good, Dr. T. I think this is a terrible idea.*

I stare at my phone as I shrink around the corner and flatten my back against the wall. The cool surface is soothing against my warm body. Is that sweat rolling down my back? I'm not too far away in case they call my name, but the small crowd of waiting patrons seems to have pushed my anxiety over the edge.

So, I close my eyes and take deep, calming breaths. I know that Dr. Trina will text me back when she is available. She could be in session right now. So, I wait. I clear my mind and breathe.

*Deep breath in, hold five, exhale slowly, do it again.* By the time my phone dings, I feel marginally better.

Dr. T: *We talked about this. Your reasons for going are solid. What are your concerns?*

Kelsey: *I feel like something terrible is going to happen if I go. I feel... danger, doom, dread.*

Dr. T: *It sounds like an emotional response to a trigger. Just remember your feelings are not facts. Our minds lie to us all the time. You'll likely be just fine if you go. Remember you had expressed it would give you an opportunity to reconnect with your family. But it's also okay for you to change your mind.*

I read the last sentence and stare off into space. *It's okay for me to change my mind.* It's such a simple concept that I never learned growing up. Instead, I brought the mantras I heard my parents say so many times into adulthood:

*Let your word be your bond.*

*Your yes needs to be your yes.*

*Follow through no matter what.*

No matter what... even at the cost to myself.

My gut is churning. It's telling me that something is

very wrong. *Our minds lie to us all the time.* I had already spent quite a bit of time and money working through some of those lies from my childhood trauma.

Kelsey: *How do I know when my mind is lying, or my gut is telling me to run away because there is danger?*

Dr. T: *Thinking about worst case scenarios to protect yourself is a coping mechanism you no longer need. Your life is good now. Ask yourself if what you are feeling is genuinely in the here and now or if it's past trauma trying to resurface.*

"Kelsey!" a barista calls my name, and I turn the corner, shove through the small crowd, and grab the hot drink with my name on it. Dr. Trina is right. Catastrophizing and conjuring up situations to fear so I'll be on my guard and ready to protect myself at a moment's notice don't serve me anymore. I have to learn to distinguish between emotional reactions and actual danger. I heard Casey when she told me how much she missed me. She said this would be a great chance to make new memories now that we are all grown up.

*We can form new relationships,* she said. I do want to be a part of that.

That is why, when they call my row for boarding, I get on the plane to fly to the isolated cabin in the Montana mountains. The place where my role was the annoying older sister. I can feel myself reverting to my childlike state already. I don't wanna go.

# FOUR

CASEY

**7 Days to Christmas**

I am bouncing on my seat. I freaking love road trips, and this one is a whole new experience. Brax surprised me with train tickets. I've never taken a train, and it's amazing. It's true that I adore all travel and new experiences, but an adventure by train far exceeds them all.

I fell in love with traveling and Brax on the first trip we took, right after I got my license to tattoo. I had never connected so completely with another person. Maybe it was the newness of the relationship or the experience in a place I'd never been, but I knew then that Brax and I were meant to be.

Brax gets me. It helps that he's an Aquarius, which is

my perfect soulmate pairing. It could not be more obvious that the universe brought us together. He loves to surprise me with weekend trips to get me out of town. I own my own tattoo business in a trendy uptown parlor in the middle of the busiest street in town and I have no problem getting walk-ins. I'm also able to take off when I want. Still, Brax has to drag me out of the shop to get me to go with him. He's good for me like that. I make my own schedule, and since Saturdays are a big walk-in day, I close every Sunday and Monday to spend time with him.

But he's never surprised me with a train trip until now. I grab his bicep and pump it a few times, squeezing hard, knowing he's strong and can take it. Some people change after they get together, but I'm as attracted to Brax as when I first met him.

Brax raises his eyebrows at me.

"Look at the view!" I squeal.

"Case, calm down. If I would have known you'd be like this the entire trip I wouldn't have—"

I playfully smack his arm. "Shut up. Yes, you would have. You love when I'm excited." I let go of his arm and rub my head against him like a cat and he laughs while he reaches down with his other hand to pet my long, brown hair.

"You're right. I would have. Over and over again. I'll buy you train tickets any time just to see this." He smirks and palms my face gently. Then he puts an arm around me tugging me closer. Like he's going to get me to sit still that long. I smile to myself. I look out the window and catch my reflection. Despite my excitement, I can see how tired I am. I'm just glad I haven't been sick.

"We need to talk about your family." Brax says as if reading my thoughts. I sigh as I feel our playful energy shift.

"Brax." I push away from him. "What is there to say?" I hate confrontation, and he dislikes my family. Not all of them. He can tolerate most of my siblings, but he really hates Kelsey. I try to think of a way to switch the subject. Maybe a little risqué make out session on the train would take his mind off it. I put my hand on his thigh and suggestively move it upward while I wiggle my eyebrows at him comically.

Brax catches my hand to stop my movement. "I know what you're doing."

I smile sheepishly, move my hand, and sit upright. "Fine."

"It'll be better if we bring it up right away. Like ripping off a Band-Aid. We need to clear the air with them before any more *misunderstandings* occur."

By misunderstandings, he means dramatic outburst brought on by jumping to conclusions. It happens a lot in my family. Brax and I have been together for seven years, and it's only gotten marginally better. When we were first together and told my parents that Brax and I don't believe in marriage and we would be cohabitating happily ever after, it caused a rift. Yep, my parents are old school. They have a happy marriage and didn't understand. I get it.

But marriage is for two people who come from stable backgrounds, and I'm too jaded for that. I was in the foster system for a few years. I saw plenty of marriages that weren't happy. I saw husbands abuse and disrespect their wives. I saw wives choose drugs over their relationships. The only reason I turned out the way I did was because I landed in my home with my adopted parents and siblings. We formed our own family.

That's not the only circumstance that made me realize the universe is on my side, and it always will be. My parents were killed in a car crash. I survived. I was a lucky child, and that luck has carried me into adulthood because I've followed the signs that led me on this path. When you look for them, you can find them everywhere.

"So, let's talk. Your family owes me an apology. Your sister owes you one. And I won't rest until that happens." Brax crosses his arms over his chest, and his eyes turn that dangerous shade of black which drowns out the brown in them when he's angry. Angry Brax is a sight to behold.

I rub his forearm. "Hey." I make my voice gentle and soothing, placating him to calm him down. "I'm not sure you're going to get an apology, and I don't need one. I love my sister unconditionally. Clearly, she's working through something emotionally." *Right?* I stare off into the distance, marveling again at the beautiful mountains that are flashing by the train window at top speed. I have often wondered what made Kelsey resurface the way she did only to be so hateful. The only explanation I have is that it had nothing to do with me, and it was something she was going through.

Brax yanks his arm away. "I'm not messing around, Case. This needs to happen."

"Or what?" I challenge him.

"Or they'll miss out."

"We can't keep our secret from them forever, Brax. They'll eventually find out."

"Oh, we can, and we will." He clenches his jaw.

I resist the urge to roll my eyes. He reminds me of a caveman when he gets like this. There's no reasoning with him. But he would never keep me from my family.

"What are you going to do, *make them* apologize?"

"Yes."

"How?"

"I'll club them over the head," Brax announces.

I would be horrified if I thought he was serious. "No, you won't."

"Fine, I'll set the house on fire."

I smack his arm. "Stop it. Thad's a firefighter. He'd just put the blaze out."

"Seriously though, your family's gonna freak." Brax grins suddenly, and it changes his whole countenance. He's so handsome when he smiles, it takes my breath away.

"Yeah," I nod and answer slowly. "It really is important that we're together on this. You're going to have to make peace with Kelsey."

The truth is, I miss Kelsey a lot. When we were little, we'd pretend we were twins. We were the same age, and since we didn't tell people we were adopted, everyone was mystified by that, even the teachers. So, we told people we were fraternal twins.

I didn't think about how weird that was until I got a little older and heard what had happened to her sister. Then, the whole twin thing seemed disturbing. Was she trying to replace her murdered sister with me? Even now, the thought makes me shiver.

"No, I don't. And I won't until she apologizes." Brax is serious. "She needs to fall in line."

"We have no choice," I insist. "My health demands it."

"But no one gets to know until everything is settled."

I sigh. "Whatever, are we done now?" I walk my finger back up his thigh. "Because this conversation has gotten super boring, and I need to burn a little energy."

Brax's eyes turn a different color. I can see the brown of his eyes smolder with lust as he hauls me onto his lap. I'm straddling him, and I'm thankful that we have our own train cabin. As I kiss him deeply, I feel satisfied that I distracted him from the subject, and I got what I wanted in the end.

You don't have to be married to know how to control your partner. It's one of the things I love most about Brax—how controllable he can be.

# HELENA FREE PRESS

## DECEMBER 15, 2012

### ASSAULT AND BATTERY WITH TWO COUNTS OF THEFT

Sixteen-year-old Braxton Sheffield was charged with assault and battery of an officer as well as two counts of theft. Sheffield was caught red-handed stealing several packages off the porch of a neighborhood home in Helena Heights. When confronted by the officer, Sheffield took the officer's baton and used it against him, hitting the officer multiple times, breaking several of his ribs. Sheffield will serve time as a juvenile offender for six years. Parents Robert III and Bonnie Sheffield, law-abiding public servants, had this to say regarding the sentence: "We would never condone violence or theft and, while we are saddened by our son's behavior, we do agree with the sentence and apologize on behalf of our son. Such behavior is appalling, and we believe in punishment for bad behavior. We feel, in this case, the consequences are fair. Thank you to our justice system for the hard work of keeping us and the citizens of this community safe."

# FIVE

## KELSEY

**7 Days to Christmas**

"Attention ladies and gentlemen, the captain has turned on the fasten seatbelt sign and has asked that you stay in your seats until the sign turns off."

From the amount of turbulence we are experiencing in the air, I'm going to guess those winter advisory wind gusts have decided to come early. The plane is descending when the captain warns us that it's going to be a rocky landing. I'm trying to figure out what that means when the plane touches down and seems to bounce on the runway.

Concerned, I look out the window and notice the direction the plane is heading is not straight ahead. We are sliding. The other passengers on the plane seem to notice as well, and the noise level drops to a terse silence. I clutch onto the armrest until my knuckles go white. I can see another plane up ahead, and I try not to imagine what will happen if we slide into that plane. Others must realize the same thing as there's a collective gasp in the cabin. How bad would the damage be to collide on the runway? I'm in the middle of the plane, so I hope the damage is minimal. But, then, my life has never been that easy.

The plane makes a crunching noise and grinds to an abrupt halt. Just like that, all the muscles I had tensed to embrace for impact relax. I didn't even know I was clenching them. The passengers start clapping spontaneously. I let out the breath I had been holding. My heart is racing. Maybe this is the reason my gut was churning before we left. Relief floods through me.

"Ladies and gentlemen, we apologize for the rough landing. It's a balmy twenty-nine degrees out there, and the National Weather Service has upgraded the storm to a winter storm warning. You can expect dangerous winter weather in the next twelve to thirty-six hours. Be careful and stay safe out there," the pilot admonishes.

I don't listen as the stewardess jumps up and starts her spiel, thanking us for traveling with her airline, inviting us to choose them again next time, and bidding us safe travels. I immediately hop up and grab my carry-on. If there's ice on the runway, there's ice on the roads, and I am traveling up a mountain. It'll be tricky if I wait too long. I need to get to the cabin before my Uber driver determines it's not safe to drive anymore. The last thing I want to be is stuck in a generic hotel at the base of the mountains for the Christmas holiday.

I'm able to procure an Uber in record speed. I assume this guy wants to make as much money as he can before the storm hits. Hating to add time to the trip, but knowing I cannot show up empty-handed, I have the driver stop at an Albertsons on the way. I get groceries I know I will need for the week and throw in some healthy snacks to have on hand while I'm visiting. I can't assume Mom will know my dietary restrictions. It's one of the many things that has changed about me since I left.

It's past four in the afternoon when the Uber driver finally chugs into the driveway of the old remote family home. As the man gets out to grab my luggage, I pull out my phone to pay on the app. A circle appears and the app spins. As I wait, I sit in the backseat, staring at our family vacation cabin all decked out in bright Christmas lights. A big, unique wreath with a bird's nest and realistic speckled eggs in it sits at the bottom, while mistletoe and bright, red bows adorn the top. One of Mom's originals, I am sure. I smile. It's beginning to look a lot like Christmas.

We call it a cabin, but it's more like a large two-story home built out of sturdy logs, authentic to the area, surrounded by acres of woods. The rustic, old-fashioned look takes me back to my childhood. The altitude is 10,113 feet, and, apparently, the cell reception is crap. I reach into my wallet and pull out enough cash to cover his fee plus a generous tip. It was slow going there toward the end. Fat snowflakes started falling halfway up the steep hill, barely covering the thin layer of sleet winter had thrown down prior to that. He'll have to take it easy getting out of here.

I jump out and offer him the cash. At his look of displeasure, I wave my phone at him. "No service. Sorry, I'll have to pay you in cash."

He hands me my carry-on, nods a couple times, scoops the cash out of my hands, and gets back into his car.

"Be safe," I call after him, feeling bad about his trek down the mountain.

Suddenly, I'm alone in the woods. There's something special about the first snowfall. The new-fallen snow under the trees sparkles with an untouched, pristine quality. It's my first of the season, so I take a moment to listen to the quiet. It's the kind that is uninterrupted by cars zooming around, loud music pumping, and obnoxious shouting. That is important because nothing unravels me like people shouting. Here, there is true silence. I'd forgotten how peaceful it is. I stand still until a gust of wind picks up, and my cheeks sting from freezing temperatures whipping around me. I can hear the leaves on the trees rustle.

I watch as white falls from the sky and sticks on the cold ground. In the time it's taken to get up the mountain, a thin layer of snow is coating everything. The thought crosses my mind that I might be standing out here because I am reluctant to go inside.

"Who has made it here?" I mumble, looking around for cars, but seeing only one. It's a station wagon called *Old Faithful* that we would now call *vintage* because it dates back to my childhood. Hard to believe she's lasted this long. Either I'm one of the first, or everyone else Ubered up here, too.

I walk toward the front porch, relishing the way my brown hiking boots crunch on the ground with every crisp, snowy step I take. I tell myself I have no reason to be anxious. I've studied dysfunctional families, and I know ours isn't the most extreme case. Not that I should compare. The things I learned in my program about why people use comparisons... let's just say, a huge number of books have been written on the topic.

Each one of my siblings has her or his own story of

trauma. I only remember some of mine. Because it was my field of study, I did my research, and I know more about my brother's and sisters' lives prior to adoption than they probably do. It explained a lot. Mom never allowed us to talk about the past. It was forbidden. Like she wanted to have this Pollyanna home where all bad was forgotten, clean slated, and we had a future of rainbows and unicorns awaiting us. All we had to do was agree to forget the past. While the past doesn't have to define us, it can give us a key to understanding why we are who we are today. It was the number one thing Mom and I fought about.

I test the front door and find it open, of course. Why would it be locked? My family does not understand boundaries. I walk in and notice the smell of fresh cinnamon rolls and coffee. My stomach rumbles. I don't even eat pastries anymore, but the familiar scent brings me back to a time of warmth and love.

"Ellen? Is that you?" Mom comes around the corner with excitement in her eyes. That expression changes to one of confusion when she sees me. "Kelsey?"

I ignore the pain in my heart that zings over her reaction. *It's not Ellen, your favorite, biological daughter, it's just me—Kelsey.* Before I can say anything, I hear fast footsteps, and my dad comes barreling into view. My carry-on forgotten by the door, Dad picks me up and swings me around. When he puts me back down, he looks me up and down with a sparkle in his eyes.

"Look at you! All grown up. Marney, look! It's Kelsey!" Dad shakes his head at Mom and pushes me forward, toward her. "We didn't know you were coming, honey. You know how your mom is with surprises."

I smirk as I recall a surprise birthday party Dad threw for her one year. We thought she was going to land in the

ER that night. It took ten minutes with a paper bag to calm her down. But why didn't she know I was coming?

Mom shakes herself from her stupor and steps forward. Her hair has turned a shade more silver, and there are more wrinkles around her warm brown eyes—laugh lines. "Kelsey, dear. It's lovely to see you. I'm so sorry. It's just that Ellen was supposed to be here hours ago, and I haven't heard anything from her... How was your flight? Come on in here. I have fresh cinnamon rolls."

I sit on a barstool at the island in the cozy kitchen. Everything is just as I remember it. The wood on the outside of the home also accents the inside. The same red flowered curtains ruffle at the top of the window. An old-fashioned picture of a cup of coffee in a colorful mug with steam spelling out the words *Latte Love* hangs above the refrigerator.

Mom points suggestively at the rolls.

I point to a full pot of coffee that's still percolating. "Just coffee, please."

Mom pours a cup with a small frown. "Cream and sugar, still?"

"Yes, please." Despite my earlier hurt feelings, I can't help but feel pleased that she remembered. "Why didn't you know I was coming? I thought Casey was going to tell you."

Mom looks around and finds her phone. She picks it up and looks at it with a click of her tongue. "We have terrible reception up here..."

"Plus, I wanted it to be a surprise," Casey says, suddenly standing right beside me.

I'm off the barstool in a flash, whirling to see my sister. She came to my graduation when I got my master's a few years ago, but it's been too long. I'm always happy to see her. Casey was always pretty, but she's really grown up and come into herself since I last saw her. Her long brown hair is pulled back into a ponytail. She's wearing leggings, a sweatshirt, and a mischievous smile. Her skin is glowing—or maybe that's the excitement radiating off her. She pulls me into a hug while my dad laughs heartily beside us.

"Looks like we're in for some trouble with these two around!" he booms. Dad was always tall and imposing, but now he seems a bit stooped. And is he walking with a limp?

"Dad!" I flush, feeling my face get red like it used to when he would tease me as a child. I'm a grown adult now, but somehow my dad still has the same effect on me. His teasing was life and death to my teenage heart. It was how he showed love.

"Don't forget about me!" I hear a deep male voice before I see him walk into the kitchen.

"Thad!" I step away from Casey and stand on my tiptoes as my brother leans down to hug me. Easily six foot three, Thad has to duck often and has always had what we tease are *tall guy problems,* ranging from hitting his head on doorframes to walking into tree limbs. It looks like he's put on some muscle mass, which makes sense for his job.

I pull away and look at him. "Fighting fires agrees with you!"

He runs his fingers through his thick dark hair, as his matching brown eyes assess me. "It better since they just made me the chief of the station!" He grins, bragging unashamedly.

"What? That's amazing! Congratulations." I grin back, easily catching the excitement. I suspend my previous concerns.

"It's so good to see you all under one roof!" Dad pipes up with a grin.

"Not all of them are here." Mom gives him a dirty look.

"Of course." Dad looks properly chastised. They've always had this dynamic. Dad is positive and upbeat, where Mom is more of a realist. They balance each other out that way.

I look around the room, casually trying to see my siblings' significant others. "Where, uh, are Melly and Brax?" I know I need to have a conversation with Casey about Brax soon. But for now, it can wait.

"Melly's upstairs asleep. Long trip," Thad explains.

Mom presses my cup of coffee into my hands, and I thank her. I look into her eyes but notice how they quickly dart away. Is she that worried about Ellen?

"And Brax?"

Casey jerks a thumb over her shoulder.

I lean around her and see him parked out in the living room watching a football game. My stomach turns. I always thought there was something off about Brax, but I chalked it up to a few instances where I saw him be sharp or border-line rude to my sister. I've never been impressed by his rough behavior. He wears an attitude like the world owes him something.

"Hey, Kelsey," Brax says, his voice barely audible over the sound of the game.

He doesn't seem thrilled to see me, but that's okay. There's no love between me and Brax to begin with. I don't think I've ever been his favorite person.

"Hey," I call back, acknowledging him. He and Casey aren't married because they chose a live-in partnership over a traditional marriage. But he has been in the family for seven years and a fixture on Casey's arm the whole time. I suppose he's earned the right to be here, as much as anyone. I just hope Casey takes the news I need to tell her well. I push that from my mind for now.

Instead, I compliment the massive Christmas tree in the corner of the living room. I smile to myself. The tree has gotten progressively bigger compared to our first Christmas here. Back then, it was a three-foot pine. Today, the tree is so tall, the star at the top brushes the ceiling. It's full and opulent. Mom did a beautiful job decorating it. Red, white, and blue ornaments with realistic red and blue birds are spaced perfectly around the full tree with white twinkle lights. But my favorite are the tiny matching bows.

"The tree looks nice, Mom."

Casey nods in agreement, but then an awkward silence falls.

"Do any of you have reception up here?" Mom asks. She's staring at her phone. "I swear I had some earlier."

We all pull out our phones.

"Not me," I say.

There's a chorus around the room echoing the same sentiment.

"Maybe the storm coming in is affecting the service?" Dad suggests.

"You're really worried about Ellen, huh?" I ask Mom.

Mom clicks her tongue. "She said her plane would land here this morning."

Alarm floods through me. It's after four in the afternoon. I glance out the window. The snow is really coming down now.

"Maybe there's a spot somewhere out there we can get reception," I think aloud.

"We can take the snowmobile." Thad raises an eyebrow. "I'll take you."

"Aren't there two?" I counter.

"One is down and out," Dad explains. "Out of commission."

"Under the weather," Mom adds.

"Done-zo," Dad confirms.

I groan.

"I pulled out the one that works and gassed it up a couple days ago. It's beside the shed, under the awning. The keys are in it." Dad points in the general direction.

"Come on, sis. For old times' sake. It'll be fun." Thad pretends to punch me in the stomach.

"I remember the last time you drove. You tried to kill me on that thing. I'll drive," I assert.

Thad thinks about it. "Compromise. You drive there, and I'll drive back."

"Deal. But I need to put on warmer clothes." I slam the rest of my coffee and grab my carry-on. I race up the stairs to my old bedroom before I wonder where is *there*? Where are we going to find cell service? Thad must have an idea. Concern etches through me as I slip on an Under Armour base layer under a hefty sweatshirt and jeans. Thad's plans always used to get us into trouble.

I wonder if we are heading straight into trouble now.

# GLASGOW NEIGHBORHOOD NEWSPAPER

JULY 25, 2015

## A MATCH MADE IN MONTANA

Congratulations to Emmeline Barnes and Thad Caper, who were married in Glasgow, Montana, on July 25, 2015. This newly graduated couple was voted *Most Likely to Be Married* by classmates. Theirs is a fairytale romance mixed with years of successes and award-winning achievements. Emmeline took first place with her clarinet solo at the District I Jazz competition, led her softball team to victory in state championships as the pitcher in slow pitch, and received her certification to be an Emergency Medical Technician her senior year. Thad was number one in All State Track & Field for long-distance running and will be taking his test to become a firefighter in September. Join me in congratulating this ambitious couple in one more success. We wish them luck for their future.

# SIX

## THAD

**7 Days to Christmas**

I lied about Melly sleeping upstairs. She's up there in my room, but I don't know what she's doing. Truth be told, she and I haven't talked for a very long time. Our marriage has been over for years. We've just been too competitive, too desperate to beat the odds to officially call it off. I suspect she's met someone else, but I don't even care. My heart belongs to the station. The place I've sold my soul to.

Getting promoted to chief made it all pay off. Melly didn't care. She just stared at me with those dead, unemotional eyes and mumbled a half-hearted *congratulations*. I was beyond the point of being worried about her. I used to suggest maybe she should go to a psychiatrist and figure out what was making her so unhappy.

She snapped that it was me. I was the issue. We've finally decided it's time to let go of this miserable, emotionless prison that has become our matrimony. I don't hate my wife, but the days of us working through our issues are so far past, I can't figure out what made us cling to it as long as we have.

We're waiting until after Christmas to tell the family that it's over. They love Melly. At times, I wondered if they loved her more than they loved me. They do adopt stray people into this family, and Melly was no exception. She fit right in. When we met in high school, she was a mess. Her family consisted of drug and alcohol addicts. Her parents didn't seem to know where Melly was half the time.

Melly moved in with us after Kelsey moved out. She took Kelsey's old room. Not that she stayed in it. I proposed to her after a pregnancy scare. Her doctor thought she was pregnant, but her body just wasn't ready. So when her period hit full force, signifying the pregnancy was over, it was too late to take back the proposal. We've been together ever since. My family is going to be devasted when we tell them our marriage is over.

I should feel the same way, but I don't. I'm relieved. Maybe I can just work my job and live my life free of guilt since I'm not trying to *fill Melly's cup,* as some book suggested. I almost shake my head, but I realize the conversation is still flowing around me.

I scan my family. Mom and Dad look good—like they haven't aged since I left the house to train for firefighting school. Casey and Brax seem to exude happy vibes everywhere. Those two might have the right idea. Why get married when you're perfectly happy together as is? I wish my marriage had half the passion their partnership has. *No.* It's too late for regrets. Regrets are for missed dinners due to unexpected emergencies. Not for the abrupt end of an era.

Then there's Kelsey. If anyone has me beat in the unhappiness realm, it's her. She puts on a good show, and maybe it's so pronounced because she's been gone for so many years, but she's frail—a little too thin—pale and unhappy. She smiles, but it doesn't reach her eyes. They look flat and lifeless. She's always been pretty, so maybe that's how she hides it. But I know the sister I grew up with, and the Kelsey standing before me today is different.

I'm different too, I suppose. I'm just a little better at hiding it. The things I've accomplished since I left home are impressive. It's how I identify myself. I work hard, and it's paid off. But I've also seen some shit I can't unsee. Fire is dispatched for every emergency, even murder. I didn't know that when I signed up, and I wasn't prepared for it. But Chicago is the murder capital of the world. I've now seen so many dead people, I'm desensitized to it. Melly would say I'm dead inside.

Speaking of which, I could go put on warmer clothes too, but I'm avoiding my beloved, and I know the feeling is mutual. We just need to get through this trip and go our separate ways.

*Maybe I am dead inside.*

# CANYON CREEK MONTANA PRESS

JULY 20, 2005

## WILLIAMS FAMILY FIRE

Thaddeus Williams II, along with his wife, Belinda, were killed when an electrical fire sparked in their home due to faulty wiring, causing a small explosion to occur. Their eight-year-old son, Thad, managed to climb out a window and sustained no injuries. His reaction to run to the home of his nearest neighbor saved his life as the rest of the home went up in flames in his wake. "I'll never forget the look on little Thad's smoke-charred face when I opened the door that night. It's horrific to lose your home. It's worse to lose your parents and find yourself alone in the world," said next door neighbor, Bertha Bellington.

# SEVEN

## KELSEY

**7 Days to Christmas**

Having drawn the short stick, I am on the back of the snowmobile. Thad is driving, and I'm hanging on for dear life. To be honest, I can't tell if he's driving too fast or not. My mind has been replaying a time when we were twelve or thirteen and Thad, well into his rebellious years, opened the throttle with me on the back. It would have been fine, but he hit an unseen tree root, which flipped the snowmobile.

We were lucky. Both of us were thrown, landing far away from the flipping machinery in a pile of fresh snow. But the fall did jolt my back. To this day I haven't admitted that my back wasn't as hurt as much as I claimed. I really hammed it up to punish Thad and get extra sympathy from my mom. To say my trust in Thad's snowmobile skills is shaky is an understatement.

"When's the last time you drove one of these things?" I ask.

Thad smiles over his shoulder. I catch the mischievous glint in his eyes. "Afraid I'm gonna flip it, aren't you?" he yells back at me.

"Umm, yeah!" I answer.

"Fighting fires isn't my only skill, you know," Thad yells back. Thad is proud of his profession. It has never occurred to him that, psychologically, he's rushing into a fire and saving victims as a way to rewrite history. It's like he's saving his parents in every successful rescue, which is a way to right the world when he didn't have the power to do so at his young age.

Holding onto the grips beside my seat, I glance at my phone and notice I have a few more bars showing service. I tap on Thad's back, and he slows the monster machine.

We are at a clearing where there aren't as many trees, and we are far enough away that we can't see the cabin. I'd estimate we are three miles from the house. I survey the ground, shocked by how much snow has fallen in the short amount of time I've been here—inches, and it doesn't look like there's any end in sight.

Thad turns off the machine and pops off, his feet disappearing under the snow. I smirk at his surprised expression but bring Mom's phone out of my pocket. We took that one since it's most likely Ellen texted Mom. Sure enough, there's an unread text from Ellen.

Ellen: *Flight delayed. I'll stay in a hotel until the weather lets up.*

No, *love you* or *I'll be fine* to reassure Mom? That seems odd to me since I know Mom and Ellen are incredibly close. They always have been. Something about the wording of this text seems off to me. Then again, I haven't talked to Ellen in years. I was never that close to her, though she tended to cling to me a bit. She's about six years younger than me. I blame it on the age gap.

I hand the phone to Thad and watch his eyes move left to right, reading the text. He hands back the phone.

"Okay, great! Good. She's fine. Let's get back. It's freezing out here!" Thad says, ready to jump back on the beast.

"Wait." I bite my lip, still contemplating. "You think that message sounded like Ellen? It's so abrupt. No greeting or *I love you...*"

Thad gives me an impatient look and shakes his head. "You're reading into it. You always do this."

Instant irritation floods me. I am trained in conflict resolution. Saying the words *always* and *never* is often a trigger. It explains why I want to lash out at him right now. Instead, I take several deep, cleansing breaths. Then a quick and easy solution enters my brain.

"Let's call her. I'd feel better if I could hear her voice."

Thad hesitates, but then says, "Geez, Kelsey, you're right. We should make sure she's okay."

Using Mom's phone, I press the call button and put the phone on speaker. We listen as it rings several times and then goes to voicemail. Ellen's perky voice says, *Hey, it's Ellen. I hate voicemail, but feel free to text me.* Then there's a beep.

Thad shrugs. "Well, we tried. Maybe she doesn't have her ringer on."

I nod, feeling sure that's it. But I text her from Mom's phone to try once more.

Mom: *Hey, Elle. It's Kels. Just checking on you. Bad reception up here, but we'll try you again in the morning. Be safe, sis.*

The cold shakes have set in, and from the looks of Thad, he feels the same. Cold but satisfied, I know that we did our best to talk to Ellen. Maybe the snow will let off tomorrow and melt a little.

Hopefully, she'll make it home in time for Christmas.

# EIGHT

THAD

**7 Days to Christmas**

I hesitate before I turn on the snowmobile. Maybe this is a tactic to distract Kelsey from our deal that it's her turn to drive back, but I turn to my sister.

"Hey, Kels, I know it's really cold out here, but I just wanted to say something before we head back."

"Okay," Kelsey responds, her eyes clouded in curiosity.

"It really is good to see you. It's been like what four, maybe five years?"

Kelsey nods slowly and crosses her arms over her chest. I can feel the wall going up, and disappointment makes me speak quickly. I don't want her to shut down on me.

"Please don't misread my intention here. I'm not trying

to make you feel guilty. I'm just saying I missed you, and it looks like time has been good for you." I try to come up with words that will draw a bridge back to me and my sister.

Her tone is suspicious. "What do you mean?"

"I mean, it seems like you've really accomplished a lot."

"So have you, Mr. Fire Chief."

"Yeah, I guess we've come a long way toward bettering ourselves professionally and all that." I grin at her. "But how are you dealing with the past?"

"Are you asking me to comment from a psychological standpoint, or is this brotherly concern?" Kelsey is making me work hard here.

"Shit, Kelsey. I guess I'm saying lately, I think I'm struggling with things from the past that I've never dealt with, and I'm starting to wonder if it's affecting my life. You run into that at all?"

Kelsey shrugs as her eyes search mine. Then, something in her face seems to soften, and she lowers her voice as if she doesn't want it to be overheard. "Are you talking about family issues?"

I shrug back. "That and maybe... other things from our past."

"Oh." The lines in Kelsey's face harden and she seems to be erecting those walls again. Okay, so Kelsey clearly does not want to talk about her trauma.

I try again. "So, you know how mom never let us talk about our lives before we got brought into the family?"

"Yes!" Kelsey exclaims with an eyeroll.

"Well, I think that wasn't very healthy, and I think it's something I've carried with me into adulthood." I shift, feeling uncomfortable, but it's not from the position I'm sitting in. I hate talking about my feelings.

"In what way?" she asks.

"Well, I'm uncomfortable talking about anything from the past. I can't even talk about what happened two days ago."

This can be a real problem since I can be on a shift for up to forty-eight hours. I'm thinking about Melly, and all the arguments we got into before I left for work that never got resolved. For the hundredth time, I ask myself if I'm the problem in our marriage. I'm not the most introspective or deeply philosophical guy, but I've had plenty of time in quasi-isolation at work since becoming chief. The chief gets his own living quarters, and there's a distinct separation from my men that is nice, but it gives me a lot of time to think.

Kelsey doesn't push which I find odd considering the profession that she's going into. Instead, she's nodding along, like she knows exactly what I'm saying. "I learned in my program that an inability to process the past means we will have a hard time going forward into the future in a healthy way. I always argued with Mom that it was better to talk about everything from the past and get it in the open."

"Oh, I remember those arguments." I grin wickedly. Some part of me loved when she was the one in trouble, not me. "I also didn't get why it mattered that much. But now I know it really does."

"I think so." Kelsey eyes me suspiciously, again.

I sigh.

It will be nice when my sister can have a conversation with me without trying to analyze my motives. But given that we've spent so little time together—and basically no time as adults—it's understandable. I also wonder if she can sense that I'm holding back the reason why I'm talking about this. Melly. I'm not ready to talk about her at all.

Maybe in the same way that Kelsey's sister's murder is off the table for her.

"You know, I'm no therapist." I incline my head toward hers. "But if you ever want to talk about yours, I'll talk about mine."

Kelsey smiles suddenly. It's as if I catch her off guard, because she says, "I wish. It's something I've never been able to talk about with anyone, not even my therapist."

I feel my jaw unhinge. "Really?" The station had a therapist come in on a routine basis to talk through any trauma in hopes of warding off PTSD. I talked through some of my childhood. It's uncomfortable talking about feelings, but someone like Kelsey, who is educated in the field, should see the value in talking about the loss of her sister.

"Really," she confirms. "I have little memory of it. It's a time in my life I cannot recall when I try. Don't get me wrong, I still have nightmares about it to this day."

"That sucks!"

"Yeah," she agrees. Now she's staring off into space and her eyelashes flutter, reminding me of the nickname we gave her when we were younger for this exact reason. Huh, I really thought she'd grow out of that. Then she says something that shocks me, and I have no choice but to take it to heart for myself.

"I'm not happy. I really thought pursuing a degree in psychology would help me figure out why. But there's a part of me that wonders if I'm just too broken to ever expect such a fairy tale as happiness."

I'm staring at her because of what she's admitted when she seems to come back to herself. Her eyes widen as if she's playing back what she just admitted. "I don't say that to just anybody, you know. In fact, I don't know if I've ever said it out loud to anyone."

I identify with what she said. Deeply. "Well, if it helps, I'll tell you that I feel the exact same way."

She smiles sadly. "It does, thanks."

"Just call me Doctor Thad."

"Ugh. I would never. Some people work hard for their PhDs, you know," she groans.

"Yet I just helped you have a breakthrough in under an hour." I wink obnoxiously.

"As much as I'm loving this brother - sister moment, it is insanely cold out here and we should get back," she responds.

I agree and don't even fight her when she reaches for the keys and switches spots with me. I'm lost in my thoughts on the way back to the cabin. What if I could process some of the past hurts between me and Melly? I wonder if my marriage would be salvageable. Well, do I even have a chance at happiness? I quickly shut that thought process down.

I don't have the luxury of hope.

**7 Days to Christmas**

Ellen won't make it home for Christmas. I know this is true as I stare out the window and see the snow falling. I can't help the disappointment that has settled in my heart. The plan was for all of us to be home for the holiday. I have very important news, and I plan on telling everyone when we're all together.

It's the kind of secret that would put me smack dab in the center of attention. I'm not trying to steal Ellen's gone-missing thunder. It isn't about that at all. I can see why Mom is so worried about her. Ellen is the baby. But even the baby grows up. I swallow the irritation I still feel over Mom's reaction to baby Ellen, convincing myself my frustration is not because Ellen is the biological daughter. She's an adult now, and her destiny is in her own hands. That is to say, the universe will decide her fate. I just hope she follows the cues it gives her.

Sudden hands capture my waist, and Brax leans down to whisper in my ear. "Rather convenient your sister no-showed."

"What do you mean?" I push his hands away and whirl around, feeling surprised by the venom in his tone. He and Ellen always had a great relationship—not that I ever understood it. They couldn't be more different, but somehow, they connected in a weird brother - sister sort of way.

"Exactly what I said." His eyes are dark and angry. "No one has to apologize when there's a nice, fake family emergency happening."

"Ugh, that doesn't even make sense." I turn away and storm to the bedroom. Okay, maybe my actions are a bit exaggerated, but my hormones are way out of whack lately. "How can you make this about you?"

Brax follows me into the room. He's barely shut it when he has me pushed up against the door. He grabs my wrists and pins them above my head with one of his large hands.

"God, you're hot when you're angry." His other hand circles my waist possessively, and his lips trace a path from my earlobe to my neck.

I can feel the anger slipping away from me. Did I mention that Brax knows how to play the control game just as well as I do? His hand moves from my waist up under my shirt and his warm palm emits heat as he finds bare skin. I groan, spurring him on. His hand moves higher, and I gasp as he cups my breast. His lips find mine and from there, our movement becomes frenzied, as if we are desperate for relief and the only way to do that is to relieve each other of all articles of clothing.

Then, Brax lowers himself down to his knees and trails his hands down my thigh. Goosebumps erupt over my skin. When he gets to my knee, he bends my leg, placing it over his shoulder.

I moan loudly as his tongue finds his intended target. Brax is good at many things, but this tops the charts. It only takes a few minutes for me to find my release. I'm not exactly quiet about it either. Maybe I should be mourning the loss of Ellen not showing up, but I can't think about that right now. This is everything.

Brax stands and picks me up. He tosses me on the bed like I weigh nothing. I'm so turned on and ready for him, he slides right in. Then he's moving with a pace and intensity that I recognize because this is how it is every single time. Seven years hasn't dulled our sex life. If anything, it's only made things hotter.

I can feel him getting close. My hands grip the comforter as pressure starts to build in me again. That's the thing about Brax. He's not a one and done kind of guy. It's not uncommon for me to go several times. He pumps a few more times then grunts hard as we both climax loudly together. Afterward, he collapses on top of me.

"Freaking amazing, baby," I whisper as I cuddle into him for just a minute before I hop up and start looking for my panties.

"Wait, where are you going?" Brax whines. "Come back here."

I'm tempted as I pause and scan his hard, muscled body. He's lying there on his side ready to envelop me to his bulky body. His arm is flopped casually over his head, and I can see the word *Blinker* tattooed across his ribcage in blocky Old English. I asked him once or twice about it, but it's one of the things that shuts him down. He says he got it when he ran with the wrong crowd as a teenager. But I can't imagine who would give a teenager a tattoo like that. I also can't imagine that it would look this good twelve years later. While it's in black and white, and it's possible since Brax isn't one to be in the sun all the time, my suspicions were never satisfied. He's lying. I know he is. After so many years, I know his tells. But I can't prove it, so I let it go. But looking at it now brings back that irritation I felt early on, when he wouldn't just be straight with me. Every time I look at it, I wonder what else he's hiding from me.

"There's no time to cuddle. My family is out there. Just a quicky for now. Cuddle later—"

Brax growls and tries to manhandle me back down to the bed. I playfully smack at him and dart away as I pick up my leggings and pull them on. I giggle as he comes at me looking like a giant bear. He looks scary and intense, but this is a game we play. I move just out of his grip as I grab my sweatshirt and throw it over my head.

This affords Brax the perfect opportunity to catch me, and I shriek loudly as he forcibly pulls me back to bed and cuddles me into his chest. I melt into him for half a second.

"Later!" I protest, pushing against him.

"Now!" He's grinning but determined.

There's a thump outside the room, and I realize with a start that my family might be able to hear us. Without thinking, I jump up and yank the door open.

Melly is standing frozen. Her cheeks are pink, and she looks like she just got caught red-handed. Doing what, I couldn't say.

"Were you listening at the door?" I'm half teasing until I

see her eyes roam to Brax, who I realize a little too late still isn't wearing any clothes as he lounges on the bed.

My eyes narrow at Melly. Jealousy floods hot into my chest. I snap my fingers at her to direct her attention back to me. "See something you like, Melly?"

Her eyes dart to mine and her mouth is open like she was going to say something but changed her mind. I move to stand in front of her, hiding Brax from her view.

"No, I'm sorry. You guys are very loud," she finally recovers.

I lean in closer. "Gee, sorry, Melly, we'd invite you in, but I don't think Thad would approve."

"That's not—"

I slam the door in her face. I was just messing around. Despite how shameless we are about our love life, we are monogamous. But as I turn back to Brax, I don't like the lustful look in his eye. Honestly, it makes me wonder if I truly know him that well at all.

"Put some clothes on!" I bend down and throw his jeans in his face.

"Hey!" he protests.

"And keep your eyes where they belong," I snarl.

CHAPTER

# TEN

THAD

**7 Days to Christmas**

When Kelsey and I return from our snowmobile adventure, I climb the stairs to our bedroom with a sense of dread. My goal with this vacation was to avoid Melly as much as possible. But my clothes are wet, and I'm cold. A hot shower would be nice right about now. The cool thing about this cabin home is the bathrooms that attach to every room in the house. We don't have to leave the bedroom or share with other family members.

I take a deep breath in and open the door to my room. I don't know what I expect when I walk in, but it's not my wife wearing tight distressed jeans that hug her curves or the white tank top that clearly shows me the outline of her

60

nipples. She's not wearing a bra. She's wearing a bit of makeup, and her short brown hair has a messy, wavy thing going on that makes it look like she just had sex.

I shut the door to the bedroom, surprised that I'm instantly hard. "Jesus, Melly. What are you wearing?"

She's standing at the window and looking outside as she casually turns her head to me. She looks down at herself. "Oh, I wanted to be comfortable."

I turn away to be respectful. If she starts wearing those kinds of clothes this week, it's going to keep. I grab a pair of sweatpants and a T-shirt, then go into the bathroom and shut the door. I start the shower and step in, letting the hot spray warm my cold body.

It doesn't occur to me to lock the door, but I'm still surprised when Melly slips into the bathroom. She's not wearing her comfortable clothes anymore. She's naked. Before I can process what's happening, she opens the door to the shower.

I can't help the way my eyes roam down her body. She's still smoking hot. She always was. My fingers flex, and I realize how badly I suddenly want to touch her. Where is this coming from?

"Mind if I join you?" Her voice is silky and full of suggestion.

"I don't know if that's a good idea—" My words die suddenly as she shuts the shower door and sinks to her knees. Her mouth is on me, and I can't even speak for half a second. I haven't had sex in longer than I care to admit, and this isn't going to last long.

As her big brown eyes look up at me, something in me snaps. Call it unawakened desire, but I pull her up and stare at her. Then I kiss her roughly. I pick her up and she wraps her legs around me. I push her back to the shower wall and sink myself into her, groaning loudly. I can't help myself. It's been a really long time. She lets her head fall back, baring her neck to me. I trail kisses down to her collarbone.

"Yes," she hisses, spurring me on.

I'm like an animal, taking what I want. Maybe what I've wanted for a long time. I'm not easy or gentle and from the way Melly is looking at me, she loves it. What's gotten into her? Have we ever been this into sex before?

Whatever is happening, I'm on board. It's like explosive sensations of lust and love happening as we both climax together, and I slowly let her down, her body pressing against mine. Her feet touch the floor, and I lean down to kiss her.

I'm at a loss for words. I can't remember the last time I kissed her. Let alone when she allowed me to touch her like this. I lean my forehead against her. "What was that?"

Melly puts her hands on my mouth. "No more talking. Talking doesn't fix anything. This..."

Her fingers trail down my body. I'm muscular in ways I've never been because there's a gym at the fire station, and when other people sleep, I work out.

"This is all I wanted for years. For you to *see* me like this. Treat me like you wanted me. To come home and ravage me."

Her fingers trail down between my legs and I'm getting hard again. I look at her, surprised by the way my body is reacting to hers. She doesn't want to talk. I guess that means I can't ask her about the rumor I heard that she's having an affair. Either I don't want to know, or I don't want to ruin the mood.

Maybe if this is what we do during our last weekend together, like a last hurrah, I should just embrace it and give her the best send-off possible. Without taking my eyes off hers, I turn off the water and reach for a towel. I wrap us both inside, pressing her body up against mine. Her skin against mine is one of the best things I've felt in years. It takes me back to the first time we were together—a first for both of us—when we fit together perfectly. But as we fall onto the bed for round number two, a pesky thought runs through my mind.

In this moment, is Melly thinking about me or someone else?

# GREAT FALLS MONTANA NEWS

SEPTEMBER 9, 1999

### FATAL CAR CRASH LEAVES ONE ALIVE

Life came crashing to an abrupt end for Carolyn and Michael Quinn, who were killed in a drunk driving accident at approximately 1:15 a.m. Their vehicle rolled multiple times, crashing into and mangling a guardrail. Upon arrival at the scene, EMTs assumed all passengers in the vehicle were dead. That is, until they heard a small child cry from the car seat in back of the car. "We quickly pulled the girl out and had an EMT look her over. Three-year-old Casey Quinn was unharmed. At least that's a silver lining in a long, horrible night," Rescue Chief Bower commented. "Numbers mean something. Today is 9-9-99. She's a little miracle child."

# ELEVEN

KELSEY

**7 Days to Christmas**

Another loud peal of laughter dominates the small living room where we all sit reminiscing about the good times. There is an accumulation of gifts stacked under the tree. Big and small packages are amassed on each other, and mismatching wrapping paper clashes in a way that's pleasing to the eye. Casey, as usual, has everyone in stitches. She always was the life of the party.

There's a crackle from the fire in the wood-burning stove in the corner of the room. Casey is curled up next to Brax. Her thin arm, covered with a full tattoo sleeve, is resting on his leg. He has his arm around her shoulder and holds a beer with his other hand. I detest drinking. I thought Casey did, too. But maybe that was one of those things she said so she and I could "twin out" as we used to call it.

The pang of not having a twin sister never seemed to go away for me. Casey always indulged my need to have someone so close to me. We learned how to finish each other's sentences. We laughed at the same jokes and wore each other's clothes. We were the same size, and a joint wardrobe gave us more options. Even into adulthood, I still feel a sense of abandonment from my real sister's abrupt departure. It's a sick thought that I push away.

Thad and Melly are cuddled up on a pile of cushions on the floor. He's sifting his hand through her hair, and she's resting her head on his shoulder. Of all the relationships in the room, theirs is the one I envy the most. Only Thad and Melly could make me want what I don't have. Mom and Dad aren't even sitting together. Dad is in his armchair, and Mom is next to me on the loveseat. This is preferable to the yelling matches they had that punctuated our moments of peace growing up.

"Then there was the time that Kelsey had this idea—"

"Let me stop you right there and say all bad ideas in our childhood started with this one." I jerk my thumb toward Casey.

"Oh no you don't!" Casey insists, her voice getting louder. "This was one hundred percent yours. Thad had only been here for what? Three days?"

"Barely five," Thad corrects with a big grin on his face.

I groan, knowing exactly where this is going. My stomach turns as I remember the outcome of this story. I couldn't sit for days. I shift uncomfortably as I remember her hand on my backside. I glance at Mom and she's frowning. I run back Casey's words and realize what set Mom off.

She likes to pretend we were always there. That we spent our entire childhood with her and Dad. But we didn't. One time I proposed that we all have "arrival birthdays," and Mom was livid. How dare I suggest that any day other than my actual birth date be celebrated?

"Anyway, Kelsey gets this wonderful, awful idea." Casey pauses with a Grinchy smirk on her face. "She takes all the cushions off the couch—"

"You were there, too," I protest, feeling childishly petulant.

"Fine. We take all the cushions off the couch and tell Thad about the *Earthquake Game*." Casey laughs out loud, her fingers making quotes in the air.

"Wait! I don't think I know this one," Melly says as she whips around to Thad. "Why haven't you told me about this?"

"Ugh," Thad groans. "It was not my finest moment."

"So, Thad lies down, like a good little brother. Then we start piling up the cushions on top of him. Thad goes—"

"Are there cushions in earthquakes?" Thad deadpans in a little boy voice.

We all laugh.

"Kelsey says, 'Uh-huh, now lay still, this is the calm before the storm,'" Casey whispers. Then she raises her voice in a crescendo. "Before Thad can answer, Kelsey and I yell, 'earthquake!' and jump on the cushions."

Melly gasps. "Wretched, wretched girls!"

Thad laughs. "That was just the beginning. Once they figured out they could get a rise out of me, they pranked me all the time."

"Poor baby!" Melly coddles him and Thad soaks it up. He seems happier than when I first got here.

"I would have tanned their hides if I'd have known," Mom grumps.

"You did know, and boy, did you ever tan our hides!" The words tumble out of my mouth before I have time to think better of them. The room falls into an awkward silence. No one likes to acknowledge Mom's capital punishment. It often came in the heat of the moment, and it is still something terrible to remember, for me at least.

A snore rumbles out of Dad, and we all giggle, which lightens up the tension. But his peaceful sleep reminds me of how tired I am.

"Who wants to play cards?" Casey asks, amping up the energy again.

"I do!" Several chorus around the room, and I know it's going to be a long night.

"I'm out." I bid everyone goodnight, knowing they will grow louder with every passing hour. Good thing I brought earplugs.

"I'm going to bed too," Mom says as she starts up the stairs after me. "I sure hope Ellen can get here tomorrow."

"Me too, Mom," I say, and it's the truth. Ellen and I might not have much in common, but she's still my sister. And no one deserves to be alone for the holidays.

"She's afraid of the dark, you know," Mom says, pausing on the stairs and looking nervous as she gazes up into the dark hallway off the landing.

"What?" I ask, confused by her words. My mind scrambles backward in the conversation to find the piece I missed.

"Ellen. She's afraid of the dark. She can't sleep until I go in and sing to her. I need to go sing to Ellen." There's a sudden urgency as she moves past me, climbs the rest of the steps, and disappears down into the darkness.

I'm frozen as I replay her words. I look down the stairs where my family is shuffling cards and gearing up for the game of the century. I consider going back down to ask them about it. Does Mom have dementia? Maybe they know or have seen the signs, but because I've been gone, I missed them. But Mom has always been a bit forgetful, so maybe I'm overreacting. I decide to wait and talk to Dad privately tomorrow.

Once I'm in my room, I collapse in my bed and stare at the ceiling. My family is not perfect, and while there might be some health issues looming in our future, my counselor was right. Feelings aren't facts. It's been nice to reconnect with them. And our brains *do* lie to us all the time. Which is why I'm going to ignore the sense of dread knotting my stomach right now.

Is this the calm before the storm?

# TWELVE

THAD

**7 Days to Christmas**

My parents and Kelsey have all said goodnight and gone to bed, leaving the two couples—me and Melly, Brax and Casey. We've been playing cards for an hour when everything comes to an abrupt halt. Someone finds a bottle of wine hidden up at the top of one of the cabinets. One empty bottle later, and we're all having a great time.

Until Brax puts his hand on my wife's leg. I suspected that Melly had been cheating, maybe for years. I didn't even care. Much. All that changed upstairs in the shower and then on the bed. Hope is a funny thing. All of that rekindled something in me. A desire to fight for us. To fix what was broken.

I lean forward and look Brax square in the eye. With a lowered, but deadly calm voice, I say, "You're gonna remove your hand from my wife's leg. Now."

Melly's face turns pink.

Casey sucks in a sharp breath as her eyes move to Melly's leg. She hits Brax's arm. "What the hell?"

Brax leers with a smirk on his face. But he doesn't move. Instead, he addresses Melly. "Do you want me to move my hand?"

There's a terse silence that lasts for half a minute. I wait for Melly to agree, but when she doesn't, I stand so quickly my chair flies out from under me and hits the floor with a thud.

"Thad, wait." Melly stands and puts her hand on my shoulder, her tone pacifying. "I think we need to talk about this."

"You think?" I flinch at the sound of my own voice. I'm not sure why I snap like this. Just because Melly and I had a couple extremely intimate moments, it doesn't mean all is fixed between us. There are years of unresolved hostility. Our physical connection won't fix that.

"Hey, don't talk to her that way!" Brax stands and squares up his shoulders like he's looking for a fight.

My eyes swing to Melly. She's not going to stand by me here. There's uncertainty in her eyes. "What the hell, Melly?"

"Sit down and shut up, Brax." Casey pushes his chest, but he doesn't budge.

"Is something going on here I need to know about?" Suddenly, my suspicious brain jumps into overdrive. Melly and Brax? I'd almost laugh, but over the past few years, I've found that I really don't know my wife at all.

"Nothing—" Melly starts.

"Melly saw Brax naked—" Casey blurts out.

Rage downloads into my body. "What?"

"Your sister propositioned me." Melly's chin juts out in defiance.

"What?" My gaze swings to Casey. This is the last thing I need right now.

Casey rolls her eyes. "Not for real. I was just messing around."

"Why were you naked in front of my wife?" I turn an accusatory finger at Brax.

"That's a good way to get your finger broken," Brax states calmly.

"You aren't answering my question." My voice is a sinister tone of calm. If this had been a conversation when Melly and I first arrived, I would have looked the other way and shoved away any feelings about it. It's not like I needed any more reasons to resent Melly. But the reconnection we experienced messed with my head. It made me wonder if our marriage is worth saving. It gave me hope I didn't know I needed. But if seeing Brax naked is what did it for Melly—

"Maybe you should take a walk and cool off. It was nothing. Casey opened the bedroom door before I was dressed. Melly was standing outside." Brax looks bored.

I want to rearrange his face with my fist. I always suspected my sister and her life partner were freaky, I just don't need it to be my business. And now they're bringing Melly into it.

"I can't do this right now." Pain sears through my heart, and I realize it's really over. It was stupid to think we could rekindle things. It's a hit to my ego to know that Melly hadn't wanted me after all. She'd been turned on by someone else and used me to get off.

It's then that I notice the way Brax is looking at Melly. He deliberately puts an arm around her, his hand squeezing Melly's shoulder, then looks at me with challenge in his eye.

"Stop it!" Casey shouts, her small hands balled up into fists.

My gut churns, and the painful way my wife looks at me with guilt triggers me.

Laced with all the anger and spite I hold in my heart, I speak forcefully. "Just so you all know, Melly and I are getting a divorce. So, you all can have a good time together."

I hear a gasp, and I think it's Casey, but then the room goes so silent I swear I can hear the snow falling outside.

Brax, who is still leaned in close to my wife, smirks at me. "Don't worry, Melly. You can do much better."

That's when I lose it. In two steps, I'm in front of Brax, and I do something I've never done in my life. My fist connects with his nose, and I take great satisfaction in the way his head snaps backward, his body losing balance as he falls on his ass. He didn't see that one coming. I shake my hand a little. Neither did I. Hitting another human hurt more than I anticipated. I'm surprised I've never done that before, given my profession.

Casey gasps and rushes to Brax.

Melly's hands fly to her mouth, her eyes wide in shock.

I leave with what's left of my dignity, taking the stairs two at a time. When I see the rumpled blankets and sheets on the bed, I wonder what I'm even doing here. Evidence of our earlier lovemaking is a complete slap to the face. I can't make myself sleep on the same bed.

I refuse to go back downstairs, knowing it would only

open me up to retaliation now that Brax has likely rebounded from my fist to his face. So, I make myself a pallet on the floor, using spare blankets and a pillow I brought from home. I just need to endure the next six days of this hellish vacation that I can't escape.

# THIRTEEN

CASEY

**6 Days to Christmas**

I help Brax get to his feet, then manhandle him to our room, pushing his large strong body with both arms and all my weight. I go to the freezer, find a bag of frozen peas, take it to the room, and throw it at his face. The bag hits its intended target.

"Ow!" Brax howls indignantly.

I shut the door and scowl at him. "Maybe you'll think of that the next time you fondle my sister-in-law in front of her husband."

"Soon to be ex-sister-in-law," Brax quips.

"You and I are soon to be *exes* if I ever catch you in a stunt like that again!" I hiss. I've never been so angry at him before, and I think either my recent diagnosis changes everything about the way I feel for him or his pig-like behavior is.

"Come on, Case," Brax groans as he tries to reach for me. "Haven't you ever thought about bringing someone into the bedroom?"

I step out of his reach and glare at him. "No. Jesus, what's gotten into you? We have a good thing going. Why are you trying to blow it up?"

"I'm not. I'm trying to enhance it." Brax tries to grin, but winces instead.

I can already see bruising around both of his eyes, but I don't feel bad for him. He deserved what he got, and I would have thought less of Thad if he hadn't reacted the way he did. No matter if his marriage is in the dumps, or not.

"Besides, that marriage is over." Brax wiggles his eyebrows.

"It's not over, you pig. Do you really think Thad would have punched you over her if it were really over? You and I might be though. Honestly, Brax, it's like I don't even know you." Cue the water works. Thanks to my mood swings lately, these tears are quite real.

"Hey." He reaches for me again and this time, he catches the bottom of my sweatshirt and tugs me closer. "If you really aren't into it, don't worry. You're enough for me."

I refuse to let my guard down, though I'm not sure why. Of course, I've fantasized about adding someone into our already hot sex life. But I pictured another guy and every-thing revolving around me. No way am I going to mention that to him right now. Besides, everything has changed—like our wild and carefree lifestyle.

I snatch my shirt out of his hand. "You're sleeping on

the couch for the rest of this trip, and we'll see if I forgive you and let you come home with me."

"What?" Brax protests. "No way. My place is with you. My woman."

"Oh, now I'm your woman?" I shoot back sarcastically. I wonder if this is the first time he's propositioned someone else in the past few years. Maybe he's just never done it in front of me. "Now you remember that?"

Brax growls and throws the bag of peas on the floor. He grabs me by the waist, and I don't try to wrestle away from him. I need this affirmation to feel like he still wants me, and I hate myself for it. He settles us back on the bed and slowly peels off my leggings. I let him, knowing that him making this up to me is going to be epic. Next, he peels off my panties. I'm still reluctant, but I don't have to forgive him to enjoy myself. Right?

He lays back down and settles me over his face. His tongue licks in the exact right spot. I try not to react, but a soft groan escapes me when he finds the places that trigger my pleasure. He grips my hips softly and moves them into a rhythm that quickens my impulses.

Greedily, I pump over his mouth and lips as I grip the headboard. I need this. I deserve this. Brax reaches up under my sweatshirt, finds my breasts, his thumb caressing the undersides and swiping over my sensitive pierced nipples. I climax way too quickly and come back to earth with a mixture of euphoria and lingering anger. I couldn't leave Brax if I wanted to. There's too much at stake.

"Better?" Brax asks.

I roll off him and pretend to be unaffected. "It's a start. But if I see you looking at Melly even one time for the rest of this week, we're through."

Brax gathers me in his arms and holds me pinned

against his chest. His deep, whispered voice runs shivers down my spine. "Even if you learned I was the worst criminal, you wouldn't leave. Because no one can play your body like I do."

The shiver turns ice cold because Brax is right. I can't ever leave him. No matter what he does. And no matter that I'm seeing a different side of him this trip than I've seen in the seven years I've known him.

# FOURTEEN

THAD

**6 Days to Christmas**

When Melly comes in, I pretend to be asleep. It would have worked too if she hadn't flipped on the light, effectively burning my retinas. Yeah, my eyes were still open. I guess I was banking on the lights staying off.

"What the—" I cut off my own sentence abruptly.

Melly steps over my bedroll on the floor and sits on the bed above me, her feet dangling over the edge as she peers hard at me. I have no choice but to look up into her face, which looks very angry right now. What gives her the right to be angry? My defenses rise and I sit up from my blanket pallet, scooting my back to the wall to face her.

"We're going to talk," Melly announces.

"It's too late for that," I say, and I'm not sure if I mean the late hour of the night or that it's too late to have a conversation that might save our marriage.

"No. I've allowed this for far too long, and look where it's gotten us." Melly's eyes are piercing mine. They are a pretty bright blue color, which is a nice contrast to her dark, brown hair. She was pretty in high school, but now, I think she's the most beautiful woman I've ever met.

"Where has it gotten us?" I play dumb, but I know what she means.

"To divorce court." She gets off the bed and shuffles through a drawer, grabbing a manilla envelope at the bottom, and throws it at me. I know what this is without looking at it. Even though I knew it was coming, it stings harder than I thought it would. This means she has a lawyer and has already started the proceedings.

I refuse to open it. "Is talking supposed to fix our relationship now?"

She shakes her head. "No. Now, I have nothing to lose, so you're going to hear what I've needed to say for years. Then you're gonna sign those papers."

I toss the envelope to the ground defiantly. "Okay."

She blinks like she's surprised that I agreed. "All I wanted from you all these years was your time and attention—"

"But I—"

"Stop. I'm speaking, and you can talk when I'm done." Her eyes are sparking with fiery anger, and I'm oddly drawn to her sudden passion. It's so much better than apathy.

I nod silently.

"I know you have to be on top of your game for your job. I understand how important it is. I even get that you might not have been promoted to chief if you hadn't poured yourself into the job. But I would have given anything to get a quarter of that attention. When you were home, you weren't really there. You weren't present. It's like you were replaying the shift you just came off. I can't imagine the trauma you must face every day on a job like that, especially in the murder capital of the world. But I haven't had you for years." Melly wipes a tear away.

I ball my hands up in fists. I want to defend myself, but I can't. She's saying all the things I would say if given a chance. But I can tell she's about to use them against me.

"I used to try to pick fights with you, because even negative attention was attention. The day you stopped fighting back is the day I knew you truly didn't care anymore. You refused to talk through the arguments then or when you got off work. That's when I stopped trying." Melly wipes the stream of tears that are now falling.

"And the affairs?" I hate the bitterness that lines my tone. When did my voice become so hard and angry?

Melly looks sad but doesn't break eye contact. "There was just one." She shakes her head as if to correct herself. "I don't mean to say *just* like it's not a big deal. It is, and I hate myself for it. I broke it off. I hated how broken we'd become that I felt I needed attention from someone else."

"You're really going to blame me for your bad choices?" I want to end this conversation. The pain of hearing her admit to an affair hurts so much worse than I expected it to. But I have to respect that she's not lying to me.

She shakes her head. "No, I accept all blame. I am so sorry I did that to you—to us. I'm sorry I wasn't strong enough to just coexist."

"And Brax?" I need to know what the hell that was down there.

Melly sighs. "That was all an accident. I overheard

Casey and Brax having sex, loudly. I'll admit, it turned me on. But mostly, I stood there trying to remember the last time you and I had that much fun together. And I couldn't. I was still pondering when Casey yanked the door open. Brax was still naked, and Casey asked if I wanted to join. Ever since then, Brax has been giving me weird vibes."

"Oh please!" I explode in a loud hiss of disbelief, trying to keep my voice down for everyone in the house who is sleeping. "Tell me you didn't use me because you were so turned on by him."

Melly pauses as if to choose her words carefully. "I was turned on, yes. But I couldn't help but think this void between us was half my fault. I wondered when the last time was that I initiated anything with you. So, I decided to try something new."

I really want to believe her, but hope is a dangerous thing, and I can't afford it. "That's it?"

Melly nods, but then she shakes her head. "What happened, what we did, was beautiful, amazing, and confusing. I never expected you to respond to me the way you did. And it showed me something else."

"What?" I whisper. I'm now hanging on her every word.

"I still love you." Melly is crying again. "I just want to start over."

I'm at a loss for words now. I look at the envelope on the floor. Given all she's revealed, I wonder if I can ever trust her again. It's true that I can't picture my life without her. I can't.

"Do you mean that? Do you really want to start over?" I ask.

Melly nods. "I didn't think I did. But now..."

"Did you get everything out that you needed to say for now?" If we do this, we need to take a healthy approach.

"Well, I've always wondered. Did you ever seek attention elsewhere? I mean, we didn't have sex for years." She looks afraid of my answer.

I shake my head. "There were a few temptations, but I never went through with anything."

"Why not?" Melly's blue eyes bore into mine.

I want to say something to shove her face in her infidelity like *I honor and respect our marriage.* But I don't. It wouldn't be true. "Because every time, all I could think about was you. I never stopped loving you either. Do I like you though? Not much."

Melly actually snorts.

I find myself chuckling along. It suddenly feels good to be so raw, so laid bare.

"Well, maybe a counselor might help us like each other better?" Melly suggests. She suggested counseling in the past, but I always turned her down.

I surprise myself by nodding. "I'm sorry I was never open to that before. And I can't help but think maybe we need to work on liking ourselves more as well."

"Yeah." She agrees. She looks at me with a shy expression. "Are we really doing this?"

"Well, I'm open to counseling, and we can try." I start. "But I don't trust you, and I'm sure I lost your trust along the way. We're gonna need to earn that back."

Melly nods with a fresh set of tears. "I kind of want to hug it out."

I smile tentatively and hold out my arms. Melly sinks to her knees and falls into my embrace. It feels so good to fold her into me. Like we still belong together.

I pull back and look into her eyes, resisting the urge to kiss her. We have a long way to go. But my mouth quirks up in a smirk.

"And Melly?"

"Yeah?"

"Stay far away from Brax, would you?"

Melly smiles and agrees.

Relief pours through me. For now. But I can't shake the feeling that things are about to get tougher.

# FIFTEEN

KELSEY

**6 Days to Christmas**

The nightmare hits me out of nowhere. Suddenly, I'm five years old again. I hear my sister scream in the bed beside me. Her scream is cut off abruptly. Then I feel the sharp blade against my neck.

I hold my breath. *Be brave, it will only hurt for a minute*, I tell myself. Then I think to myself, *Maybe, if I'm as still as a statue, he'll go away.*

Before I can scream, I hear the words, *Police, freeze!*

The pressure at my neck abates. I take a long gasping breath. I feel the sting of where the knife cut the first layer of my skin. The scar it leaves is so shallow I can only see it faintly. But the stinging persists. Cold wind whips around me. The air is biting. Freezing, numbing, no feeling in my fingertips.

I leap off the bed, my feet moving fast now. I shake Kammy. I see the blood, the gaping wound in her neck, so much lost blood. She needs that, so I put my hand in the thick, viscous liquid and try to scoop it back into her neck. It's not working. I'm sobbing, crying loudly. Then I cover her up so I can't see her neck wound. I press lightly.

My feet are stinging now. I'm not sure why. I look down and see snow. My bare feet are sinking into inches and inches of snow, and the bite of the cold is making them hurt.

*Why is there snow in here?* I wonder. I look up and notice I'm not looking at the ceiling, I'm looking at the sky, and it's pouring down snowflakes in my eyes and on my face.

My hair lashes me, and I shake my head because I can't see anything. It wraps around me, entombing me like a mummy. I gasp for air, but when I do, I suck it in. I put my hands up and claw at my mouth, frantically trying to remove the strands. Despite the vicious air circulating around me, I manage to push my hair off my face.

I blink several times, and that's when the scenery in front of me comes into view. I'm not asleep anymore. I turn in a circle and notice I'm outside. I'm on the lawn of the cabin home. A field of deep, white snow stretches for miles in front of me. I keep turning, taking in the view until I see the outside of the cabin. The front door is wide open. The inside of the house is dark. I don't know how I got here. Though my feet hurt and are starting to feel numb, I am frozen to the spot. My brain is trying to process this.

The longer I stare, the more my eyes take in the outline in the shape of a person inside the cabin, standing in the open doorway staring back at me. I stifle a scream. That's when she walks onto the porch.

"Kelsey? What are you doing out here?" It's Mom. "You get in here, or you're going to catch your death of cold."

I nearly fall into the snow as the tension leaves my body. I feel so relieved I could cry. I blink to clear the confusion in my mind. But it doesn't work. I don't remember walking outside. I walked right out the front door? I start scanning my surroundings one more time.

Mom steps out onto the porch and holds out her hand. Her voice is soft when she speaks. Like she's addressing a child.

"Kelsey, sweetie, why don't you come inside? Come in here where it's warm."

Though I'm starting to lose feeling in my toes, I take one step, carefully, then another step. Soon, I've made it all the way up the porch. I grasp Mom's hand like it's a lifeline. It's warm. Her eyes are soft. Her body language exudes kindness.

Unexpected tears flood my eyes. This is how I remember Mom when I was little. Mom pulls my hand, gently tugging me into the house. When I make it inside, she shuts the door. She envelopes me in a wholehearted hug. I have missed this. My body starts shaking uncontrollably. She's transferring her body heat to me, warming me up.

"Oh, sweetie, you're shaking! Sit down. Let me get you some socks for your frozen feet." She leaves.

I sink down into a chair at the kitchen table. Am I awake right now? I pinch my own arm. *Ouch! Well, that certainly feels real.* The house is dark and quiet. My eyes find the clock on the kitchen stove. It is two fifteen in the morning.

Mom returns with thick, wool socks and bends down.

Before she places them on me, she puts her warm hands on one foot, then the other.

I suck in a breath as the pain hits me. I can see from the single light Mom turned on that my feet are red. Mom keeps rubbing them until they start to tingle. Then she puts on my socks and squeezes each foot firmly.

"You know what you need?" Mom asks. She sounds like she's addressing a toddler.

I shake my head, feeling dumbfounded.

"Hot cocoa!" She gets up and starts pulling ingredients out of the cupboard. She turns to me with cocoa powder in her hand. "It's okay, sweetie. Some kids sleepwalk. It'll get better once you feel more comfortable. You're safe. This is your new family, and we love you."

Why is she talking to me like this? Then it occurs to me that Mom's brain must be stuck in the past when I was a child. Mom won't talk about the past. It's the reason we fight. She refuses to answer my questions about when I was a child. I've read about symptoms of Alzheimer's. My eyes tear up as I realize this is Mom reacting to the disease. I really shouldn't take advantage of the situation. Still, my heart beats faster when I realize the opportunity I have here.

"Do I sleepwalk every night, Mama?" I feel bad for playing the role of a child, but I'm desperate for some bit of truth. I remember so little of those days.

As Mom pours milk into a pan, she nods. "Yes, you've walked in your sleep since we brought you home. But it's okay. You'll be okay, once you settle in."

"Where did I sleepwalk to last night?" I prod.

"I found you in the bathtub."

"I took a bath while I was asleep?" I gasp.

Mom laughs. "No, no, little one. You took your pillow

and blankets and crawled into a dry tub. I found you there asleep in the morning."

"Wow, okay." I'm startled by this revelation. I didn't know this about myself.

"One night, you walked into my room and just stood there staring at me and your dad," Mom explains.

"Creepy," I say.

"No." Mom stops what she's doing and squats to look me in the eye. "You are not creepy. There's nothing wrong with you. You hear me?"

I nod wordlessly.

Mom stands and smooths the back of my hair with a look of compassion. "This is perfectly normal. You'll feel like a part of the family soon enough. Even if you sleepwalk forever, we will keep you safe."

Mom goes back to the stove and moves her pan from the burner and stirs it. I watch her as she grabs a ladle and spoons hot chocolate into two mugs. She brings them to the table and sits with me. She picks up the mug with one hand and grabs my hand to hold with the other.

We sit in peaceful silence, but I can't help but wonder if I ever grew out of this sleepwalking habit. The late night of sleepwalking, along with the revelation that I've always done this, and perhaps that I've never stopped, has wiped me out.

# GLASGOW NEIGHBORHOOD NEWSPAPER

## NOVEMBER 10, 2001

### BABY ELLEN ARRIVES!

Sam and Marney Caper welcomed baby girl, Ellen Marie, to the family on November 8, 2001. She was 6 pounds and 8 ounces with a shock of red hair and vibrant green eyes. She is the youngest of four—she has two sisters and one brother. If Ellen's quiet, peaceful nature is any indication, the Caper family is lucky indeed. "We could not be happier to bring baby Ellen home. We are so in love with our beautiful bundle of joy!" said Mama Marney Caper. Let's join them in saying, "Congratulations!"

# SIXTEEN

KELSEY

**6 Days to Christmas**

I wake later that morning to the sound of grumbling and banging around downstairs in the kitchen. I pull on a warm sweatshirt over my flannel pajamas and go downstairs to investigate the racket. As I climb down the stairs, I can see into the kitchen. Mom is making coffee, and her motions are short and jerky.

Not wanting her to feel I'm sneaking up behind her, I decide to announce myself. "Good morning, Mom," I say in a soft voice.

Mom whirls around, and her eyes narrow in anger upon seeing me. "Oh. It's you." She turns back around, now ignoring me.

Remembering the incident last night on the stairs, I decide to overlook her irritation and approach. "Can I help you with anything?"

"No! I don't need your help," she snaps.

I sigh, feeling sadness over her tone. She was so loving the last time I saw her, and this really feels pointed at me. I'm trying not to let it hurt my feelings. I watch her for a minute. She's jamming the coffee basket in the coffee maker hard enough that the frame looks a little bent.

"Mom." I gently lay a hand on her wrist and reach for the basket.

Mom jerks it out of my hand, and the basket, complete with filter and coffee grounds, goes flying, spilling across the kitchen floor.

"Look what you made me do!"

Before she can stoop to start cleaning it up, I put a hand on her shoulder. "I'll get it. Come here and sit down. I feel like you're upset. Are you that worried about Ellen?"

Mom looks like she wants to argue for a second but then nods her head and lets me guide her to the table. She sits down and I wait, sensing there's something she wants to say.

"It was wrong of you to treat Ellen the way you did," Mom says.

I process her words and try to think what she means. Ellen and I have always gotten along. Is she remembering a time in our childhood when we bickered? I don't say anything, I just wait.

"When you went to see her at work. You know how busy being a social worker keeps her. You walked into her place of business without an appointment and demanded she see you. So, she cleared her schedule and the things you said to her were awful. Just terrible, Kelsey."

Concern grows in me. This never happened. I have never gone to see my sister at work. I was at school. There are hundreds of miles between me and Ellen. I wonder where this is coming from, but instead of shutting her down, I ask for more.

"What did I say, Mom?"

"You know exactly what you said!" She is getting heated, and her voice raises. Color floods into her cheeks. Mom was always beautiful, inside and out. Her natural red hair and eyes most resemble Ellen's, which is another connection between them. Ellen was a surprise for her parents, *a gift from God*, Mom used to say.

My parents didn't think they could have kids, but they wanted them. So, they adopted kids who were in terrible situations with no parents or loving relatives and raised us in a house full of love. Both she and Dad were adopted themselves and grew up with loving parents. They weren't that upset when they first tried to have children and could not.

"I'm sorry, I don't remember saying anything upsetting to Ellen," I respond, and it's the truth. I've never gone out of my way to hurt my sister. I believe the lack of time I spent with Ellen was the most hurtful thing I've ever done, and even that wasn't intentional.

"You told her she was the redheaded stepchild who never fit into our family. You said she never would fit in, and she needed to stop trying. You saw through her *nice girl act*, trying to help children who couldn't help themselves. You said maybe she should just focus on helping herself, because she was the one who needed help." Mom finishes and stares at me with accusation. "Kelsey Kristine, I raised you better than that."

My mouth has dropped open, and I feel my eyes go huge. I've never been more shocked in my life.

"Mom," I breathe. "I never said any of that! I would never say those things. I don't even think them."

"Well, Ellen isn't a liar. She said you told her that, and I believe her." Mom starts to rise. I put my hand over hers. She stills.

I'm struggling because her words sting. How could she believe those things about me? "Mom, when have I ever been needlessly cruel?"

Mom's chin juts out, and she looks away. She's made up her mind, and I'm not sure how to change it.

"I didn't say those things, Mom," I repeat to assure her. But maybe I'm trying to assure myself. Mom is so adamant. "I've never even been to Ellen's office. I've been at school, remember?"

"Of course I remember. How can I forget?" Mom leans in and locks eyes with me. "You better not try to analyze me, little girl. You can keep your mean psychobabble to yourself."

Mom gets up abruptly and grabs a broom and starts voraciously sweeping coffee grounds.

"Mom, I said I would do that." I watch Mom's body language and decide not to step in. Then I see movement out of the corner of my eye. Dad is standing just outside the kitchen and motioning me to follow him. Curious, I trail him to his small downstairs study.

Dad waits until I step inside and quietly shuts the door.

"I swear, I never said those things," I start, hearing the way my voice whines like I'm suddenly ten years old again.

Dad holds up his hand. "Your mother is..." He sits heavily in a chair, his eyes searching the wall for the words he wants to say. "Ah hell, there are signs of early onset dementia, Kelsey. For all we know, one of Ellen's coworkers said those things to her, and your mom thought she was talking about you."

A mixture of emotions runs through me. Relief over the cleared-up misunderstanding, but fear and sadness over Mom's state of being. Then I think about the incident on the stairs last night.

"Dad, last night Mom told me she was worried about Ellen because she's afraid of the dark," I tell him.

Dad nods solemnly, which is a strange contradiction to his typical cheery disposition. "It gets worse at night. Right now, I'm just supposed to keep track of what's happening so they can properly diagnose her. They've thrown out that it might be sundowners." He picks up a journal and writes a few sentences. I assume they are in reference to what I just told him.

"Ugh, Dad, I'm so sorry! Why didn't you tell us?" Compassion for what he must be experiencing floods through me. I'm familiar with sundowner's syndrome from my studies. People with Alzheimer's get worse at night and experience increased confusion and agitation.

A look passes over his face, and I realize a second before he admits it. "The others already know."

"What? Why didn't you tell me?" I could have come home sooner. Or more often.

"You were working so hard to get your degree. We all agreed. We didn't want to distract you," he admits.

"We?" I feel anger creep up my chest.

"Now, Kelsey, don't take it personally. We just felt—"

"We? Do you all have family meetings when I'm not around?" My heart rate increases. I feel my face get hot. Anger burns through me. I stand quickly. I have to get away.

"Kelsey, come on. We didn't mean to—"

"Say *we* one more time, Dad," I snap. I have to get out of here. Now. I can't control what flies out of my mouth when I'm like this. I go from anger to uncontrollable rage. My counseling sessions have been lessons in coping to stay ahead of the anger, which has worked until this moment.

Not even thinking about it, I walk right out the front door. That's when I realize, I'm not dressed for the cold. I'm still wearing a sweatshirt and my PJs, and I have fuzzy socks on my feet.

"Kelsey, coffee's ready," Mom calls after me.

I keep walking. The rage keeps me warm in the storm. I don't feel the biting cold that hits my face. I don't register the ten inches of snow or that my feet still hurt from my outdoor walk before dawn. I watch them disappear under the snow with every step I take. I just shuffle through the white dunes. I see the woodshed sitting to the side of the house, and I adjust my path in that direction. I'm not really thinking. I'm just walking.

Finally, when I get close enough, I turn around and let myself fall back in the snow and stare up at the overcast sky that is still shaking down flakey precipitation, only now, it is in my face. I flail my arms and legs like a two-year-old and let all the rage fly out of me through my childish antics. I move until I have no energy left within me. Then I lay there, feeling defeated, small, and sad.

In this moment, I am hoping the snow will bury me alive.

# SEVENTEEN

## KELSEY

**6 Days to Christmas**

I'm taking deep breaths. Still lying on the ground, I'm visualizing a happy family who communicates and cares equally for one another. Maybe I can will that into existence. The thought comes out of nowhere. *Casey must be rubbing off on me.* I don't believe in all that universe stuff. But I do believe in breathing and meditation. I already feel my anger subsiding. I'm regulating back to a state of balance.

Now, I replay Dad's words. They assumed I was too busy to care that Mom was showing signs of dementia and Alzheimer's. *That's incorrect*, I tell myself. Dad is a simple man. He says what he thinks. He doesn't mince words, flower things up, or imply things. Dad said they didn't want to take my focus away from getting my PhD, and that's what he meant. There's no conspiracy to keep things from me. There's no reason for me to be angry. My anger was the result of a childhood trigger. The worst thing anyone could do when I was a kid was to ignore me. It made me feel like I didn't exist. That I had died with my sister. After the tragedy, I felt that way all too often. When I lost my sister, it felt like a piece of me had died, too. The quieter a sibling or parent became, the louder I got.

Large white flakes drift lazily to the ground, lulling me into a trance as I stare up at them. I'm still lying on the cold, wet ground. My inner child, who is done throwing a fit, is now feeling curious and light. I throw my arms out to the side, kick my legs out wider. I blink rapidly to clear the snow from my eyes as it falls and melts against my still warm skin. I begin to move my arms up and down, and my legs are making side to side motions. I haven't made a snow angel in what, ten years? In fact, it was right here.

I turn my head to the side and watch as white, sparkling, pristine snow drifts toward the wood pile under the shed. Maybe I'll grab a stack of wood before I head back in. I'll find my dad and apologize. But before I can rise, I notice something out of place. It's dirty and brown with a reddish tint to it. Like an ugly red river ran down the slope in the ground beside the stacked wood, then froze.

*What is that?*

My eyes follow the trail upward to find the source, and then my whole body locks up and my eyes bulge. Despite the cold, my body floods with heat, and I can feel sweat trickle down my back, and adrenaline floods through me.

From my vantage point on the ground, I can see a stiff, pale hand. The hand is connected to a torso that is partially blocked by the door to the woodshed that is cracked open. I see red hair. I realize I am not breathing right now. I compensate by taking a gasping, open-mouth breath in and choke for half a second.

Then, I'm up on my knees, and I'm crawling slowly toward the horrific scene my mind doesn't want to accept. The word *accident* floats through my mind as denial is protecting me from what I'm seeing. But as that theory forms, I see the source of the blood trail and discard it. A sleek silver kitchen knife lies on the ground next to the place where the blood path began. As I get closer, I can see into the decrepit building. There is a body lying lifeless on the ground just inside the shed. There is a slash in the neck and blood that has coagulated and frozen into a perfectly preserved crime scene.

As I finally let myself look at her face, there's no denying the eyes that are open wide in shock, the mouth formed into an *o*, and the stiff, frozen, and undeniably dead body of my sister, Ellen.

I start screaming. In slow motion, I turn to see people streaming out of the cabin and running in my direction. I remain perfectly still as I stare at the gash in Ellen's neck. This is my second sister to die in this manner. My mind flashes.

*No!* Only, I can't keep the vivid images from the night Kammy was killed from flooding back.

The dark room.

Kammy's scream cut off abruptly.

A man in the room.

His hand touches my shoulder.

Bright lights and loud yelling.

Police arresting the man.

So much blood on my sister's bed.

Me, scooping it up and trying to put it back in her.

Someone taking me away.

It's all too much. Panic floods into me. I can't breathe. When blackness overwhelms me, I welcome it, my body passing out as the first family member reaches us.

# EIGHTEEN

KELSEY

**6 Days to Christmas**

I hear their voices above me, surrounding me, before I open my eyes. They are whispering over my face. I can feel their presence as they hover over me. Someone leans in close enough to touch me.

"Do you think she did it?"

"She's always hated Ellen," comes the hissed reply.

"Now, now, I don't think that's true—"

"She would never!"

"She was pretty angry when she left the house..."

"Ellen's blood is frozen! She's been out here for hours!"

A loud wail erupts the speculation, the sound of infinite agony, coming from Mom.

My vision is funneled as I open my eyes. A blur of faces comes into view, and I blink a few times to see Thad, Dad, and Casey all leaning over me. I flutter my eyes and am immediately aware of several things. I am cold. I am wet. It is eerily silent. My family suspects that I killed Ellen.

That last thought dumps into my brain in a vicious attack. I sit up abruptly, and my upper body sways a little, my head light and fuzzy. I jerk my head to where Ellen was lying before. Is lying. She's still here. No one has attempted to move her. The knife still lies on the ground next to her.

"Woah there," Thad says. His large hand steadies my shoulder. It's warm and strong, like an anchor to this horrible new reality.

I swing my gaze to his face. I see concern and something else in his eyes. Is it fear? Of course, Thad is afraid. Everyone is. I look from face to face. Casey's is tear-stained, worried, and overwhelmed as she sniffs and wipes at her face, only for a fresh coat of grief to spill. Brax is behind her, an arm around her shoulder, holding her tightly. Melly is sitting beside Mom, holding her hand, with silent tears streaming down her face, her other hand covering her mouth. Mom's face is blotchy and swollen, and she's looking at me with horror and disgust. Dad is beside himself, ringing his hands and rocking forward and back, as he peers at Ellen's body. He reaches over and gently closes her lifeless eyes.

"Don't touch her body!" Thad snaps.

Dad jumps back and looks at Thad with alarm.

"This is a crime scene!" Thad states with a low growl. "Someone murdered my sister."

"Oh my God!" Casey wails. "What are we gonna do?"

Thad holds up his cell phone. I know he has no bars

because we've checked this before. "Does anyone have service?"

Everyone scrambles for their cell phones, takes them out, and peers into their screens. Slowly, we all shake our heads.

"Okay, I'm going to snowmobile back to the point where we had service yesterday." Thad, ever the one to jump in and take charge, comes up with a solution.

"I'll go," I say faintly.

"No!" Thad says a little too sharply.

"I didn't do this!" I flail an arm in Ellen's direction. Then I look to each family member, all of whom avoid my eyes. My stomach turns over, and I know before it happens that I am going to be sick. I lean over and empty the contents of my stomach in the snow.

"Gross!" Brax spits out as he jumps back to avoid the splatter.

I feel my family collectively lean backward with him.

"Okay," Casey says, "let's get you inside. You're shaking and your clothes are soaking. Seriously, Kelsey, how long have you been out here?"

"Not long enough to kill my sister and have her blood freeze." I groan as my stomach lurches again. This time, I dry heave. Apparently, I didn't have much in my stomach.

No one moves as they stare at me in terror. I shut my mouth with the realization that every careless thing that leaves my mouth is somehow incriminating me even though I know this isn't my fault. I didn't kill my sister. I would never.

On a huff, Thad gets up and stalks to the snowmobile. He looks around. He feels in his pockets and then looks around on the ground next to the machine. He stops, and his eyes fall on me.

"Did you take the keys?" Thad asks.

"What? No," I say. "I left them in the ignition." I know I'm a little out of it right now, but I vividly remember trying to decide if I should leave the keys or bring them inside. At that moment, Thad had turned back and said, *Leave them there. That's where they were when I got out here.*

"Fine." Thad's movements are jerky and short. "I'll hotwire it."

"How do you know how, Thad?" Dad asks.

"I'm a firefighter. I know how to do a lot of things." Thad pulls off the tank, and I see him pull some wires out and attempt to cross them. We all watch in silence when there is no spark.

Thad curses quietly and gets off the machine. He jiggles the snowmobile and listens. He turns to Dad. "How much gas was in this thing?"

"Full tank." Dad is rubbing his scruff as he slowly gets up to go help Thad.

Thad sniffs the air. "You smell that?"

"Sure do," Dad says as he bends down to look under the device.

"What the—" Thad's voice is incredulous as he lies down on the ground to inspect the machine from the bottom. "The gas line has been cut!" He tugs a wire out and shows it to Dad.

"You think an animal chewed through this?" Dad asks.

"No!" Thad spits out. His temper is getting the best of him now. He looks right at me as he says, "Someone intentionally cut the line. It's a clean cut and it was fine yesterday."

That's when it occurs to me. We didn't see Ellen here when we took our ride. She must have been here all along, but... "Did someone open this door?" I notice how the door is open wide enough that the door latch is flush with the wall of the shed when, yesterday, I remember it being shut. Did someone do this to Ellen last night?

"What?" Mom's voice comes out harsher than I think she intends. Then again, Mom was pretty mad at me even before this happened.

"We didn't see her when we went out yesterday," I say.

Thad freezes his movements and stares at me, his mind computing this new information. His eyes widen. He must realize I'm correct. This means this happened to Ellen last night or she was hidden yesterday, but someone left the door cracked. Like they wanted us to see her today. But why would someone choose today to reveal where Ellen is? I glance around at everyone, and they are all looking at me.

Our brains appear to be working a mystery none of us can solve.

"I'll walk," Thad finally says.

"What?" I ask.

"I'll walk to where we were yesterday and call for help," Thad restates.

"It was three miles before we got reception! In the snow, that's going to be hard to do. It'll be awfully cold." I try to talk him out of it.

"Well, someone needs to do something. She can't stay out here. You all move inside. I'll layer up and head out," Thad orders, jumping into action. I admire him. I bet he's one heck of a fire chief.

"Thad, take the station wagon," Dad suggests.

Thad's gaze sweeps to the old vehicle, and he shakes his head. The snow is so deep, it would take some time to uncover the tires. We can all clearly see the car is not going anywhere in this snow. Not to mention, there's a solid layer of ice underneath it all.

The family stands to go inside, but I stare at them in shock.

"Wait, what are we going to do with Ellen's body?" I whisper the thought as it occurs to me. My eyes scan the wild forest just beyond our home and this shed. There are wild animals all through those woods.

"This is a crime scene." Thad's eyes roam over Ellen's frozen corpse. "We have no choice but to leave her here." There's a finality to his voice that no one dares argue with. But my heart sinks. It seems so irreverent and disrespectful. But then, I suppose, this cold weather will perfectly preserve her in the meantime.

I stand and shut the door, which doesn't disturb where Ellen's body is lying.

Thad nods his approval, and with no other plan, we follow Thad back to the house. I stand at the door. My eyes rest on the red hand towel with a bright green Christmas tree on it that is hanging over the oven door latch. There are matching potholders on the counter next to the stove.

I bend down and remove my wet socks, but it doesn't matter because my clothes are also soaked. As I watch the water from my clothes make a small puddle on the floor, I wonder absently if maybe I'm in shock.

# NINETEEN

THAD

**6 Days to Christmas**

Everyone moves inside and now stands motionless in the living room. I think they must be in shock or awaiting further instructions. I watch as Dad steers my weeping mother into their bedroom and shuts the door. I head for the stairs to put on warmer clothes. I'm itching to go back out there and process the crime scene. It's what I do for a living. While I'm not a CSI, I've seen enough to know where to look for clues. But that's my sister out there. And I don't have to process anything to know who did this.

I'm having a hard time finding sympathy for Kelsey, because as I look around at my stunned family members, I decide that of everyone in this house, Kelsey is the one I can point the finger at. I can't quite explain why. It's just instincts, and mine are telling me she's guilty.

I storm up to my room and bundle up. As I layer on more clothes, I can see the blanket pallet I made and slept on last night. I don't have time to think about that right now. I'm moving so fast, I almost miss Kelsey standing in the hallway. She's looking at me with a worried expression on her face.

"Be careful, Thad," Kelsey warns me.

For some reason, that only makes me angrier because I don't think the danger is out there. I think it's in here. I might be leaving my family here as open targets.

I take the stairs down two at a time. I stop short when I see that my parents have come out of their room. Mom's eyes are red rimmed, but she looks subdued. I feel obligated to say something to them before I leave. Common sense isn't exactly in abundance with my family.

"Don't leave until I get back. I should only be gone a few hours," I instruct.

"Ever the hero," Brax snarks under his breath. Only, I'm pretty sure he meant for me to hear it.

I whirl to him. "Say it to my face!"

Brax steps into my personal space. "I said, you always have to be the hero."

I shove his chest, surprised to find he's a little more solid than he looks under that oversized sweatshirt. Still, it knocks him off balance, and he takes a step back.

Rage fills his face, and before I have time to process him coming at me, Brax tackles me to the ground. I'm vaguely aware of the loud exclamations and shouts around us.

Pain explodes in my face. Before I black out for half a second, I think, *That's fair*. I did punch him last night after all. I shake my head and see Dad is holding Brax back, and it's Melly who offers me a hand to stand up.

The looks on my family's faces range from shock to sadness. But I don't have time to care about that right now.

I turn and rush out the door.

CHAPTER

# TWENTY

KELSEY

**6 Days to Christmas**

When Thad bursts out of his room, rushing by, I am compelled to stop him.

"Thad, wait. Be careful out there!" I tell him, hyper aware that someone killed Ellen and, given the way we are snowed in up here, the likelihood that the killer is in this house is high. I shudder at the thought.

His eyes darken with an emotion I can't place. Is it anger? Is he mad at me? He looks like he's going to say something, but then he nods briefly, brushes past me, and stalks down the stairs, taking them quickly.

Thad pauses and addresses the whole room. He's giving us instructions to stay put. It's bossy, but I agree with him.

110

This isn't the time for us to split up. Even though I had come down a few stairs, I didn't hear what Brax said to set Thad off. But in the next second, Thad is pushing Brax, who retaliates with a full-body tackle. Brax gets a punch in before Dad steps in and pulls Brax back.

I feel my jaw drop, and I glance at Casey, whose face has turned red. I think about Brax's background and wonder again if Casey knows about it.

Thad stands with Melly's help and stalks out the door.

Brax turns toward the room he's sharing with Casey and angrily slams the door after him.

It's only then that I notice the stares of my family. They are all looking up at me with a myriad of emotions. Though they haven't said a word, I am feeling so accused in this moment. Like I'm glad no one has stones. Anger and frustration well up in me. I didn't hurt my sister. I'm not even the one who caused the most recent commotion.

"I'm going to take a shower," I mumble as I head back toward my room, suddenly needing to be anywhere but here. With them and their judgmental glares.

"Kelsey," Casey calls.

I turn reluctantly and look her in the eyes.

"Keep your eyes up," she says. "We're not losing another person today. Understand?"

Relief breaks free in my chest, and tears flood my eyes. I nod and head to the shower. Her words seem to indicate that she, at least, believes in me. It's only when I am alone and standing under the steaming hot shower that I let my guard down and cry. Really cry. With the sound of the running water, I know no one can hear me.

Ellen is dead. The image of her lying on the ground, frozen blood pooled at her neck, is not one I can unsee. I know this because it's there in my mind every time I close my eyes under the hot spray.

I turn away and open my eyes as I gasp for breath. Was I holding it? I think back, searching desperately for the last words I spoke to Ellen. In my panic, I come up blank. As if I had not known my sister at all. The thought brings on a fresh round of tears.

I lean against the shower wall and wail. Then a memory begins to emerge. Ellen had been twelve. She was six years younger than me, and the last time I saw her was the day I moved out. She was barely a teenager. Now I close my eyes and let the past come back.

*I lugged two large suitcases to the doorway and paused. The front door was open, and I could hear Dad behind me huffing as he hefted a box into the backseat of my car. I stood looking at the house, trying to memorize every last painting and picture on the wall. I knew, deep down, it was the last time I would see this place.*

*Sudden loud feet sounded on the stairs. So loud, it sounded like a herd of elephants. But Ellen wasn't known to be stealthy. She was short and thin but walked heavy. We could always hear her coming and teased her mercilessly about it. I turned and smiled as she ran down the stairs and jumped the last two in her haste to get to me.*

*"Don't go!" Ellen cried as she flung herself into my arms. She hugged me in a way that pinned my arms to my sides, and she squeezed me tightly.*

*"Ellen." I laughed. "I have to. College starts in a week. I need to get moved in."*

*"No!" Ellen looked up at me, pouting petulantly.*

*"Hey." I pushed back from Ellen so I could look her in the eyes. "This isn't forever. It's just goodbye for now. I'll be back."*

*"No, you won't," Ellen said. "You're leaving me."*

*"Ellen, I'll never leave you. I'll always be your sister. You can call or FaceTime whenever you want. If I'm in class, I'll call you back as soon as I can," I told her.*

*"You promise?" she asked, doubt in her eyes.*

*"Yes."*

*I held out my pinky and Ellen linked hers in mine.*

I kept that promise, too. Until Ellen stopped reaching out. She started driving, and her social life took off. I was busy studying for my undergrad, then my masters, then PhD.

A nagging feeling clawed at my chest. Had I placed too much importance on my education, letting a diploma outrank my family? Or worse—was it a chance to escape? As I turn off the shower and reach for a fuzzy towel, I wonder, *Was it all worth it?* I know the answer. Had I known that would be the last time I would see my sister in person, I would have come home to visit more often.

I dress quickly and run a brush through my wet hair. I feel the sudden need to be with my family. The only people on Earth who get the way I feel right now. This loss is so jarring and unexpected that every time I think about it, it leaves me breathless.

I walk down the stairs and find my family, minus Brax, sitting in the main room, silent, catatonic, and staring at nothing. The couch, loveseat, and recliners are all taken. As usual, I'm the odd man out, though Thad being gone put Melly in a seat by herself. Casey is sitting without Brax by her side. I wonder if he's still in his room, but I'm sure Casey is giving him time to cool off.

There's one lone chair, an empty wooden kitchen chair rounding out a circle. I assume they mean for that to be my chair. I don't have to assume for long.

"Have a seat, Kelsey." Mom puts a palm up toward the chair. Her eyes are hard and cold as they peer into me.

Obediently, I comply. As I sit, I look up to find every eye on me. They are looking at me with one consistent emotion in their eyes—fear.

I cross my arms over my chest, taking a defensive position. I see now. This is meant to be an interrogation.

# TWENTY-ONE

**6 Days to Christmas**

Every member of my family stares at me. One by one, I meet their eyes, looking for an ally. Someone who doesn't think I killed my sister. Mom's eyes are hard and cold and pinned on me. Her face is red and blotchy, and tears are streaming. Her body is rigid with grief and anger. I shudder inwardly. She is convinced this was me.

I look at Dad. He doesn't hold my stare. He's leaned forward with his elbows on his knees. He quickly finds a spot on the floor and glues his gaze there. My heart sinks. My dad has always been in my corner. But I can see it in his posture and lack of eye contact. He has his doubts.

I seek out Casey, who wipes her eyes as a fresh round of

tears surge. She gives me a shoulder shrug and a sad smile. I do not know how to interpret that. Casey was always quick to rush to my defense. Now... It looks like she's not committing. But then I glance at Brax, who has come out to sit next to Casey. He has his left arm around her. His body language is aggressive and dominant in the way his right shoulder is positioned slightly in front of her, his body practically wrapped around her. He's protecting her. From me.

Finally, I take in Melly, who is not looking at me. Her focus is out the window. She's biting her nails. She's worried about Thad, who is braving the cold weather while the snow is getting deeper by the minute. I think about Thad's anger toward me. Surely, he doesn't blame me for cutting the gas line, too.

Dad clears his throat, drawing every eye to him. "We need to talk."

I know that voice. Someone is in a lot of trouble.

"Ellen..." his voice breaks in sudden emotion, and Mom lets out a wail of grief.

This is wretched. Tears flood my own eyes. Ellen was so young. She had so much going for her. Who would do this? No one in this family would hurt Ellen on purpose. No one had a cause. And yet... my eyes scan my family again. We're the only ones up here on this mountain for miles and miles. The weather has gotten really bad, and the roads were slippery when that Uber driver dropped me off. There's only one car out there, and it belongs to Mom and Dad. I have my doubts about the reliability of the station wagon on the steep mountain roads.

Thad has been gone now for about an hour. If that's any indication, the ability to move around quickly up here would be impossible with the weather. Not to mention, a person could not be outside in this weather for a long period of time, limiting the person who harmed my sister to the people sitting in this room.

"Ellen has been killed," Dad starts again. This time he seems to have a hold of his emotions. "We need to get to the bottom of this."

Does he mean to play detective?

"Dad, what are you—"

"Shush!" His voice is a little harsh.

I start at his tone.

"I've always taught you all that violence is not the answer to conflict." He looks hard at all of us. When he gets to Casey, she jumps to her feet.

"You have got to be kidding me. You think one of us did this?" Casey puts her hands on her hips.

"Sit down!" Dad's fist pounds the coffee table.

I jump in surprise. Dad was never the loud one. When he was the enforcer, he would glare and his voice would get quiet, and that is when we knew to give him our full attention.

Brax tugs on Casey's shirt so she falls back down into him. He wraps his arms around her. Is he protecting or controlling her?

Melly tears her eyes from the window. Her complexion is pale, and she seems to be thinking before she speaks. "Thad would say we need to nail down the time of death. Most of us were likely traveling here when this happened."

"Explain," Brax demands.

Melly blinks at him a few times. "Ellen was due in on a morning flight. The weather wasn't bad yesterday morning. That means it's possible someone outside the family was here at that time."

"The door to the woodshed was closed, and we didn't see her when Thad and I went out on the snowmobile. That might mean that a killer was prowling around outside, moving in and out of the woodshed, and revealed Ellen's body to us when they wanted to." I am just throwing out the first things that come to my mind.

"Then, where is the killer now?" Casey says as she puts her fingers up in air quotes around the word *killer*.

"Either the killer is someone outside the family—out there somewhere—" Melly waves a hand toward the window.

"Or they are right here. In this room." Brax fixes me with a hard stare.

The room goes silent. Once again, I catch the looks of distrust angled at me. How did I become a possible murder suspect in the eyes of all my family members over the course of a morning?

"There is something we aren't thinking about," I say, a thought occurring to me. "Who's to say that whoever killed Ellen isn't waiting to pick us off one by one?"

Melly raises a shaking hand to her mouth and whispers, "Thad."

Immediately, I understand her fear. Thad is out there, trying to find a cell signal. He might be in danger. I stand and sweep out of my chair, heading toward the stairs.

"Where do you think you're going, young lady?" Mom's voice is shrill, and young me would have stopped dead in my tracks over that tone.

"I'm going out to look for Thad. We all should. He never should have gone out there alone." As I run to my room, I hear pandemonium break out downstairs. My words seem to have put them all in motion.

I layer up quickly and run back downstairs where I find Dad alone in the living room. I stop short in front of him.

He looks sheepish. "I know you didn't have anything to do with Ellen, and I think they do, too."

"Then why—"

"You've been away a long time, and I don't think it's uncertainty. I think it's resentment. It's just going to take some time to make up for that. You've changed. We all have," he explains, but it feels like he's just making excuses. I know they really do suspect me.

"But I couldn't help being gone." The words are lame even in my own ears.

"You could have come home on breaks, but you chose not to." Dad isn't arguing. He just states this as a fact. "We all just need time to reconnect."

I nod slowly, hoping he's right.

One by one, my whole family meets back up, and we make a plan to go to Thad's rescue.

I'm hoping he doesn't need it.

# TWENTY-TWO

KELSEY

**6 Days to Christmas**

The shadows are longer, leading me to believe it's later in the afternoon when Casey and I head out to find Thad and bring him back. I vaguely wonder where the time went. Wasn't it just morning when I discovered Ellen's body? The thought makes tears well up in my eyes again. I try to shake my head to ward them off, but it's no use. My tears fall.

"They'll freeze to your face, you know," Casey says as she falls in step with me. We are both bundled with multiple layers of clothing, warm shoes, and puffy jackets. We borrowed some things from the old *snow closet*, as we called it growing up.

"Wives tale," I say back, but just in case, I wipe them

away. Then I realize this is the first time I've been alone with Casey. It's terrible timing, but I need to tell her about Brax.

"Hey, Case. There's something important I need to tell you." Selfishly, I guess I am hoping this will get my mind off my emotions.

"Yeah?" Her eyes flick to me, then back in the direction we are walking.

"Do you know that Brax has a prison record?" I decide to be blunt.

Casey's eyes widen in surprise replaced quickly by a flash of anger. "Maybe. What do you know?"

I can't tell if she is trying to protect Brax or if she doesn't want to admit she doesn't know.

"When he was sixteen, he assaulted a police office after he got busted for stealing. He served time, Case. Six years. You know this, right?" I need to be cautious here. Far too often, I have been the brunt of Casey's anger. Her moods can switch without warning. But maybe that was just her as a teenager.

"How did you find that information?" Her voice is cold with a whip of emotion laced in it. Color stains her cheeks, but I can't figure out if it's because of the weather, if she is mad that I know, or if she is spiraling because she's hearing this information for the very first time.

"As part of my PhD program, I have access to documents that are sealed by the courts." I'm not a good liar, so I keep it simple. Sealed court documents are only accessible by court order. My thesis covered family dysfunction. When I was researching Brax Sheffield, I found an old newspaper clipping about Brax's arrest, but the court records were sealed. I assume this is because Brax served his time as a juvenile.

Casey is silent as we continue to wade through the deep snow. It's slow going with the depth.

Finally, Casey breaks the cavernous silence. "You never liked Brax."

I'm instantly on the defense. "That's not true."

"Yeah, it is. The first thing you said when I told you I met him and had moved in with him was, *Are you sure you know what you're doing, Casey?*"

"It all happened very fast!" I protest, but Casey is not wrong. I always thought Casey grabbed the first guy that came along because of her inability to be alone. Now that I've studied it, I think it goes further. Casey has an anxious attachment style, which means she has codependent tendencies, takes responsibility for others' feelings, and worries about her loved ones abandoning her. She might even think that if she and Brax broke up, no one would ever love her.

"So what?" Casey snapped. "We've been together for seven years. I think it worked out just fine."

"Okay." I sigh. "I just wanted to be sure you knew about his background. Assault is a big deal."

Casey's chin juts out in defiance. "I do, thanks."

I nod, then I stop. I lightly put my hand on her shoulder and look her in the eyes.

Reluctantly, she raises hers to mine.

"I love you, Casey. I just want what's best for you. I'm sorry if that has come across as critical, rude, or mean spirited in the past."

"Oh." Casey stares at me like she's never seen me before, and I materialized from thin air.

I can tell she's having a hard time knowing how to respond. I didn't say that to disarm her. I said it because it's true. I've always felt overprotective of her. Sometimes to an unfair degree.

I turn back to our task and move forward again. My eyes are scanning the white, snow-covered ground, but Thad is nowhere in sight. It doesn't surprise me. I know exactly where he was heading because it's where we went on the snowmobile. I stop short.

Casey crashes into me. "Oof! Do you see something?"

"No. You don't think he got frostbite and couldn't use his legs, causing him to fall under the snow and get buried in it, do you?" I ask, fear spiraling through my entire being.

"Jesus, Kels! Could you be any darker? No. I don't think that's what happened. Come on. He's probably fine and will be annoyed we all came out to search for him after he told us to stay put."

I let go of a breath I had been holding. "I hope you're right."

We walk in silence for miles. Well, what seems like several miles is probably one.

Casey turns and looks back where the cabin has become tiny in the distance. "Do you really think he would have come this far?"

In response, I take out my phone and check my cell service. I flip my phone toward her to show the lack of signal. "No bars yet. Yes, he kept going. Trust me, we went about three miles on that snowmobile."

Casey's eyes widen. "That's a really long way in the snow."

I nod and start walking again.

When we've walked so far that I wonder if we could hear the family if they yelled for us, I pull my phone out and check again. Still no service. I'm still staring at my phone when I hear Casey gasp. I look up as she starts running. Her run is slow and sluggish, like that dream I have where no matter how much I try to run, I can't because I'm stuck. Casey is slow-motion running.

"What is it?" I ask when I catch up to her.

"Thad's hat!" she gasps.

I want to tell her to preserve her energy because we still have to get back, but I don't. I can't speak because I see Thad's stocking cap, too. But that's not all I see. Bright red, round droplets sprinkle the snow, breaking up the monotony of white. For what seems like minutes, I stare at those red drops. Then I follow them. Like macabre bread-crumbs left for us to find the owner. The owner who I'm pretty sure is Thad.

My heart is racing, and I'm panting by the time I reach the indentation in the snow where I find my brother lying face down, clearly unconscious. The closer I get, the more the details of what I'm looking at become clear.

Blood. There's so much blood. The back of Thad's head looks dented, and a pool of blood seems to have filled it in. I hear a gagging sound as I gaze at the head wound that looks fatal. Then I realize, I'm the one who is gagging.

# TWENTY-THREE

KELSEY

**6 Days to Christmas**

Casey is standing beside me in shock, as if the snow has frozen her. I nudge her out of her trance, and she starts shaking from head to toe.

"Is he... Is he..." she stutters as her teeth chatter. I know what she's asking, but I don't know the answer, so I fly into motion.

"I don't know." I grab Thad's stocking cap out of Casey's hand and wade over to him. The snow comes up to my calves. Walking is not an easy task, but the adrenaline flowing through my body is warming me up with every step I take.

I peer down at him and turn to find Casey still stuck in place.

"Do you have CPR training?" I ask.

"Wha-what?" she stutters, trying to focus on my words.

"CPR training. Do you have any?" I'm trying to stay patient, but I am now worried about how long he has been out here face down in the snow.

"Some. It was years ago, though." She finally creeps closer.

"Me, too." I check my phone. Still no service. I place his hat on the back of his head and apply light pressure. "We're going to have to turn him over."

"Aren't we supposed to leave him where he is?" Casey asks.

"Yes, but we can't leave him face down. Plus, I need to check his pulse."

A loud wail erupts from Casey.

I look up at her. I feel nothing now. I know that I'm systematically shutting down my feelings and emotions, going into survival mode.

I summon my most authoritative voice. "Casey, I need your help. I need you to do what I say so we can make some decisions. We don't have a lot of time."

Casey hesitates, her eyes get big, and then she nods.

"Okay, you apply pressure to the back of his head, here, while I attempt to roll him." I wait just long enough for her to place a hand over the hat and press lightly. Then I get on one side of Thad, put my hand under his shoulder, and push. I grunt with my effort, but Thad doesn't move.

"Okay, you're going to have to help me move him," I tell Casey. "This is going to be tricky. You'll have to come to this side with me, hold his hat, and put your body weight into him with me. Can you do all that?"

Casey processes my words and nods. We both sink to our knees in the snow. I let the toes of my shoes find a hold on the ground to dig in.

"Okay, ready?" I ask.

Casey nods.

We both put our weight into flipping Thad. Thad isn't the biggest guy—he's pretty lean—but he is tall, and now I'm realizing that he must have been packing on muscle. Muscle that Casey and I put together do not have. It takes everything in us, but we finally get him flipped over.

Thad's eyes are closed, and his face is red from the cold. I immediately check for a pulse. For seconds, I feel nothing. Just as I'm about to give up, I feel a faint but consistent beat.

"He's alive," I say as tears spring to my eyes. But the relief is short-lived because he is still not conscious, which is a bad sign.

"Thad?" Casey shakes him gently. She takes off her gloves and puts her hands on his face. She must be trying to warm him up with skin-on-skin contact. "Thad?"

He doesn't respond. I look at Casey, and she looks back at me. We know we are in danger here. So many things go through my mind at once—*concussion, hypothermia, bleeding out.* For the life of me, I cannot remember what happens to a wound when it's freezing cold outside. Will the cold help the situation or hurt it? It can't be good. Not one thing about this is.

"We need to get him to a warm place," I say. We both turn and look at the distance from here to the house. With no phone and no vehicle, it's going to fall on us to get him home.

"How?" Casey asks.

"We'll have to drag him."

"We could barely turn him over!" she protests, her voice lilting in a hopeless wail.

"I know." I bite my lip until I taste blood. Then, with a burst of inspiration, I take my scarf off. Carefully, I place Thad's hat on his head to cover the wound while I tie my scarf around his head, at his forehead. "Maybe that will stop the bleeding."

"I don't think we can do this," Casey says, looking doubtfully back at the cabin that seems so far away.

"Well, we have to try. Maybe we can shout until someone hears us. In the meantime, we are strong, and we are determined. We can do this because we have no other choice. Are you with me, Casey?" I search her eyes for the inner strength I know she has hidden in there. Casey is a fighter.

She takes a deep breath and nods. A look of steel enters her eyes. She grabs Thad's right arm. I grab his left. We turn his body around so we can drag him backward, and the effort is staggering. We stop for a second to catch our breath. But it's on us. No one can save him, but us. We move quietly for several feet, then pause to rest.

"Now's a good time to yell and see if anyone is around, Casey." I take out my phone. There's still no signal, but I am desperate. I dial 9-1-1 and watch as nothing happens.

We are truly on our own up here.

# CHAPTER
# TWENTY-FOUR

CASEY

**6 Days to Christmas**

When we divvy up into search partners, I find myself with a real problem. I refuse to pair off with Melly or Brax because I'm mad at them both. But you better believe I'm watching them to make sure they don't pair off themselves.

As luck would have it, Dad and Brax agree to team up and go north. Mom and Melly decide to stay back at the house in case Thad returns. That leaves me with Kelsey going south. This is good news, until I remember that Kelsey looks the guiltiest for Ellen's murder of all of us. I know my family feels the same way. But in true Caper family fashion, no one is saying what they're thinking.

I walk slightly behind Kelsey and try to gauge her fat

versus muscle ratio. I'm taller than she is, and I've always been more athletic. If for some reason Kelsey turns on me, I think I could take her. Unless Kelsey has a weapon. She could have one, and I would never know.

Kelsey's gloved hands are in her pockets, which are deep. *Perfect hiding place for a knife.* Like the one that slit Ellen's throat. Or the one that slit Kelsey's sister Kammy's throat when they were five. It's not lost on me that Ellen died in the exact same way Kelsey's sister died, and I'm rethinking everything I ever knew about Kelsey.

Did I ever see an actual news story about Kelsey's family? I make a mental note to Google it later, but then I curse myself. For the hundredth time since I got here, I remind myself that we have no Wi-Fi, and my phone is useless up in the mountains. But right now, I'm just wondering if Kelsey, at five years old, would have the ability to kill her entire family. She'd certainly have their trust. I mean, no one would see it coming.

I shake my head at the dark direction of my thoughts. I watch a lot of crime documentaries, and I listen to podcasts, too. But this accusation mentality isn't me. I'm positive and upbeat. There's no way a five-year-old girl could physically massacre her family, and if she did, Mom would have never adopted her. I settle back into my *give everyone the benefit of the doubt* belief. Or maybe it's just denial.

I'm uncharacteristically quiet as we walk. Typically, I tell jokes or stories when I'm uncomfortable because I hate silence. I'll do anything to take my mind off serious life situations—laugh, joke, go on an adventure, have sex with Brax—because, hey, life is too short. Only now, I can't escape the serious. My younger sister Ellen's life was cut short, which is the very reason we are out here. Because Thad could be next.

I just hope when we find Thad, he'll be alive, well, and annoyed at us for coming after him. He was so upset when he left earlier, and I know the feeling. Anger surges back into me on his behalf and my own. What was Brax thinking? I've never seen him blatantly hit on a married woman in front of her husband or me, for that matter. Maybe my diagnosis changed everything. Maybe this is something Brax feels like he needs to get out of his system. But try as I might, I can't justify Brax's behavior. I grit my teeth. I'll be shutting that down.

"Case, I need to talk to you about something." Kelsey finally breaks the silence.

I look at her for the first time since we left the house. She looks like she's trying too hard to appear casual, and her discomfort is overwhelming her. Like she's wearing pants that are too tight, and she's having a hard time breathing. She's pulled her hands out of her pockets, and she's opening and closing them quickly and erratically. Is she just cold?

I think I nod or something to give her an indication to keep talking.

"Do you know that Brax has been to prison? That he assaulted a police officer when he was caught stealing? He went away for six years." Kelsey's words are slow. She pauses between each sentence as if gauging my reaction.

But her words rub me the wrong way. At first, I think she must be lying. But then I think, *Why would Kelsey lie about that?* Also, I asked Brax when we first got together, jokingly, of course, if he'd ever been to prison. It was during that awkward do-you-have-any-skeletons-in-your-closet phase when we were getting to know each other. Brax told me *no*.

I can't admit to Kelsey I have no idea what she's talking about, so I go with it.

I clear my throat. It's suddenly very phlegmy. "How did you find out about that?"

She answers, but I don't hear her. My head is suddenly roaring with anger. Kelsey wouldn't make something like this up. What if Brax really had gone to prison? Why, did she say? Assault and theft. I realize with a start that there's a lingering silence.

"You never liked him." I blurt out the first thing that comes to my mind. At first, Kelsey is defensive. Then, the strangest thing happens. She apologizes for the times she shamed me or made me feel less than. I stare at her in shock. I don't know what to say. Kelsey has never apologized to me. Ever. It's nice but uncomfortable at the same time.

I think about informing her that Thad and Melly are getting a divorce just to change the subject, but I don't. Then I wonder why he wants to divorce Melly. I always thought they were solid. I never would have teased Melly had I known. God, I hate thinking we might have been part of the problem.

I glance at Kelsey, wondering if she heard our fight last night. She must have. I rarely feel ashamed, and I will not apologize for my lifestyle choice to not get married. But suddenly, I wonder if that's a problem. Maybe Brax isn't as committed to me as I thought he was. Maybe Brax isn't who I thought he was at all.

Kelsey is doing that weird blinking thing she used to do when we were kids. Rapidly fluttering her eyes while she spaces out and moves on autopilot. I'm about to nudge her shoulder to get her to stop. I hate when she does that. It creeps me out. But then, I reason, maybe she's trying to blink snowflakes out of her eyes. It's really coming down out here.

We've been walking a long time, and I'm starting to feel tired. What if Kelsey is leading me out in the middle of nowhere to hurt me? I can't even allow my brain to say what I'm really thinking. *Murder me.* I shake my head to rid myself of thoughts like that.

I turn and look back at the house. I try to keep the nervousness out of my voice. "Do you really think he would have come out this far?"

"Yes. We drove almost three miles yesterday on the snowmobile before we got service—"

"Three miles!" I interrupt. I don't think I can make that.

I don't hear anything else she says because after walking a little farther, I see something in the snow. With shock, I recognize Thad's gray stocking hat. It's dusted with snow, but it's clearly his. I cry out and point.

*Oh my God!*

There's blood. My stomach turns over, and I almost heave into the snow. The sharp contrast of clean white, crystal snow with the red-brown blood is jarring. There's no way Thad is alive. I look in the distance, but I don't know what I'm looking for. Is someone out there picking us off one by one like some horrible joke that we don't know the punchline to?

We're standing out in the open. I peer hard into the tree line that borders our property. It's about ten steps from where we are. The forest is thick, tangled, and wild. Despite the lack of leaves, it would be easy for someone to hide in there.

My eyes fall on Kelsey. Or is the danger right here,

closer than we could ever imagine? I go through the motions of following Kelsey's every command, and before I know it, I'm helping her half drag, half carry Thad back to the house.

Kelsey said he's alive. So, why is there such an intense sense of foreboding settling in the pit of my gut? We're not okay, and we're not safe. Someone wants us dead. I'm convinced we are all in danger.

"... yell, Casey." Kelsey's voice cuts through my viscous thoughts.

I open my mouth and obey, letting my loud voice bellow into the stillness. "Help! Dad, Brax? We found Thad!"

I think I yell three more times before the guys show up seemingly out of nowhere, and they relieve me and Kelsey of dragging the heavy weight of Thad's body through the deep snow. I always heard that muscle weighs more than fat, but I never believed it until now. My brother has always been fit. Melly must be an idiot if she thinks she can do better than Thad.

I should be focused on Ellen's murder and on what appears to be an attack on Thad. But in my haze and inability to form coherent sentences, my mind keeps coming back to one thing.

Melly better keep her hooks out of my life partner.

# TWENTY-FIVE

## KELSEY

**6 Days to Christmas**

Casey and I are using all our strength to move Thad through six inches of snow, and the effort is making my legs burn and my arms shaky. We have no choice but to keep going. No help is coming for us—we're it.

When we stop, I double check the scarf. The blood is starting to seep through. My heart rate picks up, and panic sets in. Casey drops Thad's arm and lets out a shuddering breath. She covers her face. Is she crying?

"I can't," she wails. "He's so heavy. Is he going to make it?"

I wonder the same thing, but I can't say it. I need to be strong. I take a deep breath in and summon my inner calm.

"Casey, we have to keep going. No matter what. It's his only chance of survival." My voice breaks on the word *survival*, but I grab his arm and look back at the house with determination in my mind.

Casey drops her hands, looks at my face, and nods. She wipes her eyes and picks up Thad's other arm. We shuffle walk again until we can't anymore. I check Thad's pulse. It's faint, but Thad is alive. He has remained unconscious through all of the jostling. I can't help but think it's not a good sign. Tears blur my vision, and I too wonder if Thad is going to make it. I can't lose another sibling. At the thought of Ellen, my composure slips. I give myself a few minutes, letting the sob overtake my body. Then, I pull it together, wipe my eyes, and take a deep breath in.

Finally, after dragging Thad about half a mile, and fifteen minutes of Casey yelling, Brax and Dad appear and spring into action, slow-motion running. It would be comical in a normal situation, but nothing about this is comical. Or normal. Thad might die. He's in critical condition. We all know unconsciousness with a head wound, in the cold, is bad.

Brax and Dad take over. Brax grabs both of Thad's arms, and Dad takes his legs. They move him the rest of the way to the cabin much faster than we could. We follow behind, thankful for the reprieve. At least, my arms are.

We fling open the front door, startling Mom and Melly, who are sitting together at the kitchen table. Upon seeing Thad's unconscious body, Melly cries out and launches to her feet. Thankfully, she's a nurse and has worked as an EMT. She immediately starts barking commands.

Mom stands and covers her mouth, which has dropped open in shock. Her wide eyes land on me and narrow in blame. My heart falls. I remember that she doesn't believe

I'm innocent. Today, my mom is my accuser, and I can't remember a feeling that has ever hurt me more.

I take a deep breath and turn to follow the men into the bedroom at the foot of the stairs. It's the room where Casey and Brax have been staying, but it will be easy to move belongings around. It would have been too difficult to carry Thad up the stairs. Plus, we need to reduce the amount of movement in his current state.

"We need clean sheets," Melly commands.

Mom flies into motion.

Melly points upward. "We can use our blankets from our room upstairs."

I move quickly, running up the stairs. I gather their comforter, a blanket, and pillows. I run, or waddle fast, back downstairs and watch as they tuck the sheet in tightly. The guys lay Thad on the bed. Melly takes the blankets from me and lays them on top of Thad's still body.

"Kelsey?" Melly's eyes find mine.

I snap to attention. "Yeah?"

"We need a clean towel," she orders.

I run to the linen closet, grab a navy-blue towel, and return. I hand it to Melly and watch her undo the scarf I had tied around Thad's head. I watch her face go white as she views the wound. I know it must be bad, but then, it is likely impossible for her to keep her face objective. I don't have to look at the injury again to know it is bad—the kind of bad that is not accidental. Thad was hit with something—hard.

"I'm going to have to clean it up to assess how bad it is," Melly says, her eyes drifting to me. She gives me a list of supplies to go find. It makes sense. Casey is borderline frozen. Mom is a sobbing mess. I have already shut down my emotions, so I am reacting well in this emergency.

I nod in answer to her request and scurry out of the room. I look around the kitchen. Suddenly, Mom is there. Tears are still streaming, but her face softens when she looks at me. But there is a firm determination lining her features. Gone is the confusion of last night. Her eyes are clear, and her hands are capable as she finds and hands me the first aid kit. Then she grabs clean dish towels and runs one under hot water. We both go back to the room together.

I watch Melly doctor Thad and murmur quietly to him as she works. Mom stands next to her and hands her the supplies she requests. I'm reminded of times when we were little and would scrape an elbow or a knee. Mom would gently wash the spot, then put Neosporin over it. Then she would bandage it if needed.

I stand in the doorway and lean my head against the wood. Who could have done this to him? I think back to the blood in the snow and realize there was an absence of footsteps. How is that even possible? Someone was working hard to cover their tracks. Then I realize I didn't see Thad's tracks either. Otherwise, it would have been easier to find him. Maybe they covered them by shuffling backward, duck walking through the snow, knowing the falling snow would make a solid cover before anyone came looking for them.

My eyes look out the window. It's getting dark out now, but I can see the heavy falling flakes. It's really coming down out there. It hasn't stopped since I arrived. There's easily ten inches on the ground.

My stomach churns, and maybe it's my guilty conscience, but a random thought enters my brain.

*Would this be happening if I had stayed home?*

# TWENTY-SIX

## CASEY

**6 Days to Christmas**

I watch my mom, sister, and Melly work on Thad for fifteen minutes. It's only when I feel Brax lean into me, his muscular body supporting me as if I'm leaning against a wall, that sudden anger hits inside me, and I don't want him touching me.

I move away from him and whirl so I'm looking him right in his face. I'm tall, but I still have to tilt my chin up to look in his eyes. He looks mildly surprised by my quick, jerky movements. More than that, Brax looks tired. He's a good-looking male in his early thirties who takes very good care of his body. It's rare to see bags under his eyes.

"We need to talk," I whisper snap.

A mischievous glint appears in his eyes as he reaches for me. "Yeah, okay. Let's *talk*."

I yank myself away so he doesn't make physical contact. I jerk my head, and we climb the stairs to where he and I are now staying in Thad and Melly's old room. As I shut the door behind me, I'm struck by how the room smells like Melly's perfume. Our luggage has been moved up here, but Thad and Melly's clothes are still in the dressers. We'll deal with that later.

Brax flops on the bed and removes his thick hiking boots. "So, talk."

I turn and lean against the door. "You went to prison?"

Brax sits up suddenly, his body going rigid. His tan face flushes red. His brown eyes have turned a shade of black. The stiffness of his body conveys his instant anger.

"Where the fuck did you hear that?" Brax growls.

"Is it true?" I push back.

"Answer my question," he commands.

"You first." I'm not going to lie. Brax is making me very nervous right now. He's never been physically abusive, and I can't remember when he's used his size to his advantage, but I am feeling jittery over what he might do. Now that I know he has an assault charge.

"I went to juvie. Yeah. I served my time. Those records are sealed. So, how the *fuck* did you know?" Brax stands and crosses his arms over his chest. I've never known how intimidating he was before.

It doesn't occur to me to lie, though as an afterthought, I realize it might have been a good idea to protect Kelsey. When I say her name, Brax tenses up and starts muttering to himself.

"They promised that would be sealed, and no one would ever find it—"

"Who promised what, Brax?" I ask. "I need the whole story."

Brax pushes a hand through his hair, agitation rippling off him. "My parents. My lawyer. Jesus! They promised me that once I did my time, the records would be sealed." He starts pacing. "It was such a bullshit charge anyway."

"It was assault and battery and theft," I say so he doesn't even have a chance to lie to me. My eyes are locked on him.

His eyes roam the wall just above my head. "I was sixteen. A stupid teenager. It was a dare. My friends and I were bored. Our parents left us at home all the time. So, we roamed around looking for trouble. Someone dared me to take a package. In that moment, an officer drove by."

"That's convenient," I say.

Brax looks at me and narrows his eyes. "Like it was a set up?"

I shrug a shoulder. I don't know his friends.

"Well, it wasn't. And it wouldn't have been a big deal, but the officer used excessive force. That's what a teenager can't prove. The officer tackled me to the ground and put his knee into my chest. I was a big kid. Strong, you know…" Brax looks at me.

I nod for him to continue.

"So, I told him I couldn't breathe, but he ignored me. I grabbed a baton off his belt and swung it at his ribs. I guess it was a little hard because it broke a few. But, whatever. At least I could breathe. He fell off me. But before I knew it, the cop had me in handcuffs, and I was in the back of a cop car." Brax sits back on the bed and leans his elbows on his knees, staring at the floor between his feet. I can tell his story took it out of him.

I take his hand and pull him to sit next to me on the mattress. "That's it?"

He lolls his head to the side as he regards me. "Yeah."

"Okay, because I don't need any other surprises. We have a lot going on right now," I remind him.

"Yeah. I know."

"Thing is," I start. "Didn't your family have money?"

Brax stiffens. "Yeah, why?"

"I'm just surprised they didn't get you a good lawyer. It seems like they could have given you a lesser sentence for that." Or let him off with a warning. I don't really know anything about the law. But that seems reasonable. "And shouldn't it have been attempted theft?"

"It was my parents, okay?" Brax snaps.

"What was your parents?" I wonder. Brax has a bad habit of playing the victim. I know this about him, but I also know everyone has flaws.

"They set this up. They were these upstanding citizens. They volunteered and did all these amazing things for the community. But they never had time for me. And when I got in trouble, they made it a point to tell me my punishment would fit the crime. It was the last thing they said to me before I was taken to kid prison."

"Geez, Brax." My mind is reeling. "Why didn't you ever tell me this?"

Brax lets out a humorless laugh. "When? When we met? Hey, baby, I've been to prison the past few years. You free tonight? I'll pick you up at eight."

I smirk a little. I can feel my anger slipping away, and I feel pity for teenage him, but I hold onto my indignation, wondering how much of our relationship is real. "You lied to me."

"Yeah, well, you would too," Brax defends himself.

I say nothing, momentarily stumped. I think about it. Would I tell the truth about something like this? Then I know the answer. "I would never lie or omit the truth about something that big."

"Figures." Brax's eyes narrow. "Everyone is conditional. Just like my parents."

I choose not to respond to his dig. "Did they ever come to see you?"

"Are you kidding?" Brax makes an angry sound. "They were embarrassed of me. I haven't seen them since that day in the courtroom."

"Wow." I blink slowly, processing this. I knew he wasn't close to his parents. I even knew they had had a falling out. But I was secretly hoping with my diagnosis we could try to make amends with them.

"Are we done here?" Brax asks, anger still in his voice.

I look at him with all the feeling in my heart. My eyes cloud with tears. "I'm sorry you went through that."

"You're not mad?" The anger leaves him as his eyes narrow suspiciously.

I shake my head, throw my arms around him, and hug him until he relaxes against me, melting into my touch.

His voice takes on a teasing tone. "It was so awful, and I didn't know if I would make it. Please, baby, kiss it and make it better?"

I pull back and smack his arm playfully.

"Hey!" he protests.

My eyes lock on his. I lower myself to his shoulder where I smacked him and put my lips on the spot.

"Here," Brax says as he pulls his sweatshirt and T-shirt off with one quick movement.

My fingers find and trace his *Blinker* tattoo. "That's where you got this tattoo. In prison?"

Brax nods, and I can tell he doesn't want to talk about it.

"Please tell me what it means." I press a kiss to the scripted word.

Brax grits his teeth. "I accidentally bumped into someone my first day there. He and a few guys shoved me around. Said I needed to use my blinker. We became friends. It became a thing. Got the tattoo."

I kiss a trail up his muscular shoulder, to his neck, and up his powerful jaw. Brax is nice to look at and he knows it. He moves his face quickly so his lips lock with mine. Then he hooks his arms under mine and hauls me across his body, lowering back in the process until I'm lying over his chest, my legs straddling his body.

Then I kiss away every pain, all the while putting more pressing problems to the back of my mind. A feeling of guilt niggles at the back of my mind and I wonder, *Is it okay to enjoy myself while my brother is lying downstairs fighting for his life?*

# TWENTY-SEVEN

### KELSEY

**5 Days to Christmas**

Today begins just like yesterday. But it's not the same at all. Everything has changed. My youngest sister is dead. My brother has been attacked. The list of suspects is limited to the small group of people who are in this house. With me. Then a thought occurs to me. I know where I was after Thad left, but I don't know where anyone else was. I took a long shower, after all.

After a brief shower to wake me up, I go downstairs expecting to find Mom in the kitchen like every other morning, but she's nowhere to be found. My eyes fall on the clock on the microwave. It's no earlier than any other morning, and yet, every bedroom door around the bottom floor is closed tightly. I wonder vaguely if the doors are all locked and surmise, they must be.

I make coffee and sit at the table sipping the hot liquid, not really tasting the bitter black drink as it goes down. My eyes stray to the room where Thad and Melly are staying. I've never seen more devotion or love than I do from Melly.

I'm not a hopeless romantic, and the list of men I've dated during my university days is short. No one really fit with me, and I'm not willing to compromise my standards. But that wasn't the biggest factor to relationships not working out. I'm pretty intense, and the guys I dated were often intimidated by that. No one stayed around long enough to get to know me. But then, I wondered how much *I* really knew me.

Something happened as I progressed in the field of psychology. I learned more about myself—why I do what I do, how I respond to situations, as well as my motivations. I like the focused, studious version of me. As I delved into my degree program, I realized I had found my niche. Not only did I enjoy learning about psychology, I found I was good at it. I began to apply the things I learned. Things like self-care and boundaries, while uncomfortable in the beginning, became lifesaving in the end. I wonder how much of that I have put into practice since I have been back home. Given my state of mind right now, I would assess, very little.

The day progresses the same way it starts—quietly. I see my parents and Casey and Brax a few times for meals, but then they retreat to their rooms. At noon, I knock on the door to the room where Thad and Melly are staying. In my hand is a makeshift tray with a sandwich and chips on a plate along with a bottle of water.

Melly answers the door. Her eyes are red rimmed, and her hair is disheveled. She manages a small smile for me as she thanks me. She turns to shut the door, but I put my hand out to halt her.

"How is he?" I ask.

Tears fill Melly's eyes. "No change."

Dread fills my soul. "Oh?"

She shakes her head slowly. "I don't know what else to do. The bleeding has stopped. The hit was to the back of his skull, and it's not as indented as it originally looked, but it's just a waiting game to see if he—" Her voice breaks, and I know what she's not saying.

If Thad wakes up.

I nod in understanding. I feel like I should hug Melly, but she's holding the tray of food in her hands. So, I step back.

"Let us know if there's any change or if you need anything," I say.

She thanks me and shuts the door.

I'm left staring at the wooden barrier. The rest of the day moves slowly. The wait is excruciating.

"That does it!" Brax explodes out of nowhere, startling the terse silence that has begun to define the atmosphere in the house. He storms into the living room, and from where I sit, I can see him yanking pieces of clothing off the coat rack. He's layering up and throws his coat on along with a stocking cap over his messy, unstyled black hair. His black-brown eyes are intense, and they roam wildly around the room. Casey and I follow him from the main room.

"Where do you think you're going?" Casey asks, fear in her eyes. I recognize it because I feel the same way.

"This is ridiculous!" Brax exclaims in a whisper shout. "I'm not staying here doing nothing like a sitting duck, waiting to be picked off by whoever is out in those woods. I'm going for help."

Casey's eyes widen. "You think someone out there is doing this?" Her gaze flits to the window as if she's trying to peer through the thick cotton curtain that covers it and into the darkening sky that now envelopes our mountain cabin.

"Yes," Brax breathes. "No one in this family would do something like this. We might be assholes to each other, and there's a lot of backstabbing and gossiping happening. But there's no way we would hurt each other like that."

He's wrong. Wasn't he the one who tackled Thad yesterday? I deliberately choose not to point out what Brax seems to have forgotten. In fact, there's a hint of a bruising around Brax's eyes that I didn't notice before. Did someone hit Brax when I wasn't around? Does the purple outline serve as evidence of the violence this family is capable of?

Still, I feel the passion in Brax's words, and they give me hope. Despite how I've always felt about him, it warms my heart and echoes my thoughts exactly. In this moment, I feel connected to him. I draw closer to him and Casey.

"I mean, no one is perfect." Brax turns his gaze at me and levels me with a cold look. My initial warmth fades. Why is he looking at me like that? "Very imperfect—but no one would go this far."

"I'm sorry, are you looking at me specifically?" The words pop out of my mouth before I can think better of it.

"Yes, *you*, specifically," He confirms, venom lacing what he says.

"Brax, stop. Let it go," Casey says in a soft voice.

"Let what go?" I whirl to look at my sister.

Casey refuses to meet my eye.

"Last spring," Brax starts. "Surely you remember what you said when you ran into each other?"

My mouth drops open. I haven't seen my sister for three years. Since I got my master's degree, and she came for my graduation. I shake my head, and my eyes widen as I come up blank.

"You told her her tattoos were trashy like she was, and the whole family agrees, but no one wants to say it to her face." Brax is angry and confrontational.

I'm shocked. "That never happened," I sputter, defending myself.

"Oh? You calling Casey a liar?" Brax's voice raises. His face flushes red, and his pupils have dilated, so I can only see the blacks of his eyes. He's scary like this. "Talk about causing trouble! I don't know where you and Ellen got the information about my prison sentence, but everything is out in the open now, so your attempts to sabotage me failed."

"Ellen? Ellen knew about your record?" I am trying to process one thing at a time. There are two accusations happening here.

"Yeah. You people in your professions must have access to records no one else does. But it's over and done with. Casey and I are good. So, stop trying to break us up. And stop saying mean things to my woman!"

I look to Casey to correct him. I never said the things he accused me of, but Casey's face is bright red, and she has crossed her hands over her chest. She is staring at Brax with anger in her eyes.

"I told you to let it go!" Casey hisses at her significant other.

"Casey! Tell him the truth. That never happened. Why would you make him think something like that?" I confront.

Casey's eyes snap up to me. "Really? Are you going to deny that? It happened. But you're entitled to your opinion, so I let it go. Which is what I told you to do as well." Casey pokes her finger at Brax's shoulder hard enough that he flinches and rubbed at it.

"Casey, I never—"

Brax interrupts me. "Stop. Just stop. Everyone is tired of this perfect princess act of yours. You're trouble. I've always thought so. I just put up with you because Casey loves you so much." Brax jams his hands into his coat and turns toward the door. "I don't have time for this. You two can work your shit out while I take the car to go get help. Your brother is dying in there." He points to the room where Thad is still lying unconscious.

"No!" Casey gasps, clutching Brax's hand as if to detour him from leaving and steals a glance behind at me. I am right here. Whatever she says, she has to know I'm going to hear it.

Casey lowers her voice almost to a whisper, but her words are clear.

"I can't lose you. Things are different now. You can't just think about yourself anymore."

"Actually, Casey, I'm not just thinking about myself. Don't you see? That's the point. I'm going to do something instead of sitting around here waiting for something to happen. I'm going for help." He pulls her closer and folds her into his arms.

"I can't lose you," Casey insists. "*We* can't lose you." There are tears in her eyes now. Who does she mean when she says *we*? It's no secret that the family is lukewarm about Brax. They always have been. Unless she means... It suddenly occurs to me what is going on. My eyes widen in surprise.

"What kind of a man would I be to my family if I didn't do something about this?" Brax drops his arms and steps back from Casey, really looking at her, his eyes suddenly soft. "I'll come back to you. I promise. What happened to your parents is not going to happen to me."

"No," Casey whimpers.

"Don't leave this cabin. Whatever you do, don't go outside." His words echo Thad's from earlier. Brax turns his gaze to me. "Someone needs to stand watch 24-7. If anyone tries to get in, you scream like hell and wake the whole house."

I nod. It's a good plan.

Then Brax turns, scoops the keys for Mom and Dad's station wagon off the counter, and strides out the door, shutting it behind him with firm decisiveness. I hope he knows where a shovel is because it's going to take him a while to dig out of this snowy nightmare.

Casey is crying with silent tears streaming down her face. I come up beside her and wrap an arm around her shoulder. Casey stiffens, and I can tell she's upset about what Brax brought up. I can't fathom why they think this is true. I've been away at college. I never took enough time off to go visit her. Now, I regret that. Maybe that's where this is coming from. Regardless, I can see that I'm not going to change Casey's mind. So, I stop trying. I hug her tighter when Casey attempts to pull away.

"You're pregnant," I say softly, burying my hurt over her accusation. I turn so I can look her in the eye. "Congratulations, sister."

My words seemed to startle Casey out of her silent storm of emotions. "We were going to wait to surprise everybody Christmas morning," she says quietly, her eyes dull. They keep flicking to the front window where after what seems like an hour, but is really fifteen minutes, the car lights illuminate the snowy scene outside, then they slowly disappear down the drive. I'm actually surprised

Brax was able to dig out so quickly with all this snow pinning the car in.

Now I wrap my other arm around Casey and hold her tight. Like old times. I'm happy for her while comforting her at the same time.

"It's the best Christmas surprise ever. I bet Brax will be back in time to share it with us. He'll be okay." But even as I make the declaration, my gut is telling me otherwise.

He's not going to be okay at all. None of us are going to be okay.

# TWENTY-EIGHT

## CASEY

**5 Days to Christmas**

Being pregnant is such a foreign concept to me. We didn't plan this. We hadn't even talked about if we wanted kids. I was adopted. Brax had terrible parents. When it happened, it just didn't seem real. It helps that I have no symptoms whatsoever. Some people are incredibly nauseated the entire pregnancy. I haven't even had morning sickness.

I keep calling it my *new diagnosis* like a foreign invader is taking over my body and growing there without my permission and no evidence to show for it—yet. But it's more than that. The estimated due date falls on the same month and day that I lost my parents in the car accident. I can't figure out how to interpret it. Is this a lucky date since

I lived, or an unlucky one because they died? Regardless, I've been reserving my excitement until I figure out what it all means.

Brax just thinks it's funny. I had no idea how he would take the news. But from the way his chest puffed up with pride, I'm going to say he's pretty happy about the whole thing. But this weird protective thing he's been doing with my family is new. He's never been their biggest fan. But he's insisting they all need to clean up their act, or we won't come around with the baby. I just roll my eyes. Brax doesn't get to decide that.

What I can't figure out is what he was thinking by flirting with my sister-in-law to purposely antagonize Thad. Is it possible that Brax shows me one side of himself, but is really a different person elsewhere? I sure hope not. After seven years in this partnership, I hope I've seen every dimension of him. Maybe the baby is freaking him out more than he let on. Like, he's struggling with the thought of domestic life.

For the first time since my diagnosis, I feel an intense desire to protect my unborn child, and Brax has just left me alone up here. It feels like the ultimate abandonment. What was he thinking anyway? Shouldn't he feel the same protectiveness over me and his unborn child? I sigh and realize, with a sense of fairness, that's exactly what he thinks he's doing. By leaving, he's going to get help. He feels more productive doing that than sitting around. Doesn't he realize that in doing so he has left me a target here? Especially since I can't shake the feeling that the danger is likely on the inside.

I don't know the first thing about protecting myself. I love people unconditionally, and to look at them with suspicion changes my whole belief system. A deep sense of sorrow wells in me. I shut the door to my bedroom behind me and lock it. Earlier, we carried our clothes from the room downstairs, and I'm about to load them into the dresser when I stop and stare at it, wondering how heavy it is and gauging if I can push it without doing any harm to my body or the baby.

This family vacation has turned everything upside down. For the first time in my life, I'm thinking about boundaries and how I've never had them. Maybe Brax is right about Kelsey. I should have never put up with the things she said to me. Neither should I put up with Brax lying to me all those years ago. Mostly, I'm thinking about survival. Instincts I never had to have before are starting to break through my subconscious. Maybe I should consider that everyone in this house has the potential to harm another person. And if I'm not careful, the next person will be me and this little person inside me.

I rub my stomach and try to imagine what it will look like when I start to show.

"It's you and me, baby," I whisper.

With a burst of creative solution, I take two towels from the bathroom and carefully lift and slip a towel under each side of the dresser. Then I push. The hardwood floors make manipulating the furniture easier than I expected. The armoire slides easily. I put my body weight into the dresser until it is fully blocking the door.

Only when I feel safe do I lay on the bed and stare at the ceiling. How long before Brax will make it back? An uneasy feeling settles in my stomach.

Is Brax planning to come back at all?

# TWENTY-NINE

## KELSEY

**5 Days to Christmas**

The quiet that falls over the house is anxious. We all seem to be waiting for something. Casey is waiting for Brax to return with help. Melly is waiting for Thad to wake up. I'm waiting for the next shoe to drop.

I remember this feeling. When I was first placed with Mom and Dad, I was afraid of everything. My true family was dead. Who would ever love me again? I wondered if my new family would return me if I did anything wrong, like a used toy that didn't work. Then there was the fear that the man who killed my family would come back and finish the job he started and kill me, too.

That's when the nightmares began. For years, I was

convinced the murderer was coming for me. I was trapped in this home with these nice people and no way to save them or myself when he returned for me.

*Sitting ducks*, Brax had said. What if he was right? We are all sitting up here snowed in on a remote mountain with nowhere to go and no one to help us.

I'm on the couch in the living room with my knees drawn so I can rest my chin on them, watching Casey pace around the house. She can't seem to just be still. She had sequestered herself in her room after Brax left. I had to really talk her into coming down for dinner.

"Case, why don't you put the kettle on and brew some herbal tea?" I don't actually want tea. I just think she would do better with a task. Something to get her mind off what's happening. A distraction.

She stops pacing and stares at me. I wonder if she actually is seeing me in her dazed glance. Then she nods and turns to the kitchen. She disappears around the corner, just out of sight, and I can hear her banging around as she turns on the sink faucet. I hear her set the kettle on the stove.

Suddenly, Casey screams. I'm up and running to the kitchen on pure instinct. My mind shoots a few different directions. Her pregnancy... She stubbed her toe... Someone is in the house and pulled a knife on her... But as I turn the corner, Casey is staring mutely, horror on her face as she stares out the front window.

I follow her gaze and see nothing. "What happened, Casey?"

She's pale as she points a finger in front of her. "I saw—"

"What, Casey? What did you see?" I want to grab her shoulders and shake the words out of her mouth.

"A shadow," she whispers.

Dad and Mom trickle in and hear Casey's words. Suddenly, everyone is crowding in around us, and I feel claustrophobic. I try to back up, but I run into Mom. My breath becomes shallow, and I start gulping air. I know this feeling. It's all too familiar. It's the same feeling I got when I was a kid, and the chaos of my family closed in around me. Only, I'm not a kid anymore.

I take deep breaths to offset the panic I feel and remind myself that I'm okay. I'm safe. Still, I make myself peer into the dark night, lit up only by the moon, and I don't see a shadow. Is that what we've become? Frightened adults jumping at the slightest movement we see? It could have been an animal darting around to find a warmer spot—an alcove from the still-falling snow.

Casey jumps and screams again when the kettle on the stove starts squealing—a high-pitched sound that hurts our ears and breaks our pensive silence. Mom quickly moves the kettle off the hot burner.

"Geez, Casey," Dad chides. "You nearly busted my eardrum."

Casey looks out the window one last time and looks sheepish as she turns to face Dad. "Sorry. I really thought I saw something. Guess I need to get my eyes checked."

Dad envelops Casey in a hug. "We're going to get through this, pumpkin."

Casey nods, but she doesn't say what we are all thinking.

*Will we get through this alive?*

"Should we go out there and check?" I ask.

"No!" Dad snaps. He walks over to the door and jiggles the handle to be sure it's locked tight.

"That's how people get killed in horror movies," Casey whispers. Her eyes are wide, and she's staring off in the distance at nothing in particular. I wonder when she last slept. She's seriously getting spacey.

I open my mouth to stay something, but Mom puts a hot cup of tea in Casey's hand and leads her back to the living room. She sits beside Casey, and I follow mindlessly. I stand there, trying to figure out what to do next when my eyelids start fluttering as I blank out. I remember my siblings gave me an annoying nickname because it happened so often—Blinker. I realize with a start that I haven't spaced out like that since I was a kid. It was a hard habit to break.

Sudden hands on my shoulders make me jump. I turn and see Dad there looking guilty for startling me.

"Kelsey," he says, "you need to go to bed."

"No, I—" I stop talking suddenly. I... what? What can I really do right now? "I need to stay awake with Casey." I glance at the now open door to the room where Thad is still lying, unconscious, and Melly is sleeping at his side.

"I'm going to shuttle her to bed next," Dad says. "I can take first watch."

I nod but wait at the foot of the stairs until Casey finishes her tea, and Dad helps her up from the couch.

We all go up the stairs to our bedrooms at the same time. It feels like hours before I fall asleep. My brain is spiraling. My thoughts are out of control, and I feel like they are moving in a circle, which is making me dizzy.

What are we going to do with Ellen's body? Will Thad ever wake up?

Will Brax return with help? If he does, will it be too late? Why do I feel so guilty?

# THIRTY

KELSEY

**4 Days to Christmas**

I sleep late the next morning. I'm not sure why I should get up and rush downstairs. My brother is still fighting for his life. We got lucky that Melly is a nurse. She opted not to move Thad anymore until he was stable, which is why we didn't attempt to put him in the car and take him down the mountain. That, and only Brax is crazy enough to attempt to drive a station wagon in ten inches of snow and ice.

I wondered how he's faring in this weather. I try to push down the fear that looms in my stomach. Had he made it anywhere? Maybe help is on its way as I lie here. I refuse to let my mind wander to the other possibility. The one where Brax might have slid and driven off the mountain. Or worse, he is in danger—like Thad was. And Ellen.

The thought of Ellen clenches my heart. Tears pool in my eyes, and they fall again. Her body is frozen outside, unmoved. As gruesome as that is, the family agreed that the cold would preserve her, and we mustn't move possible clues from the crime scene. Maybe Brax will bring back police and an EMT.

I roll onto my back. How has this become my life? I slowly rise and grab a pair of clean clothes and take them to the bathroom. Leggings and an oversized sweatshirt feel the most appropriate for a day like today. As I step into the hot water and let it flow down my back, I wonder, *A day like what?* What would today bring? A full-body shiver rolls over me. I am horrified by the possible answers to that question.

As I turn off the shower, I hear a knock at my bedroom door.

"Just a minute!" I yell. I dry off quickly and dress. My skin crawls over the lack of lotion, and I forgo a hairbrush in favor of expediency to open the door. My wet hair hangs in clumps, and I think it might still be dripping onto my sweatshirt. I've never felt so undone. Still, I swing the door open.

Casey is standing in the doorway, biting her fingernails. She looks small and pale. I remember when she used to do this as a child. Her shoulders are hunched forward, her head is bowed slightly, and her hands are clasped together in a prayer position just under her chin. She is making an effort to fold in on herself and appear as small as possible.

I am shocked when the thought occurs to me. She feels afraid—of me. What could she possibly be afraid of?

"Casey, what are you—"

"We need you downstairs," she cuts me off. "Thad is awake."

I gasp and forget my appearance altogether. I rush out of my room. "That's great news! Why aren't you happy about that?"

Casey puts a hand on my shoulder, stalling my movement. "I need to warn you, Kels."

My heart sinks. Does Thad have amnesia? Is he somehow worse now that he's awake? "Warn me about what?"

"Thad is—"

"He's what?" I want to shake the words out of her.

"He's saying—"

"What? What is he saying?" I stare at my sister who gapes at me, her mouth opening and closing like she's trying to speak, but the words won't come out.

"Oh, for heaven's sake!" I rush past her, down the stairs and to the room where everyone is crowding the doorway. I turn my body sideways and push myself between Mom and Dad.

When I see Thad, relief floods through me. His eyes are open, and he has a little color in his face. He doesn't look spacey or like he's not all there. He seems fine. Then, his eyes swivel to mine. I feel an instant jolt as his whole face scrunches up into anger. In fact, his whole body seems to radiate with it. Red floods into his face, and he tries to sit up, despite Melly's soft warnings.

"Stay calm." She pats his arm.

"Thad!" I feel joy, but I'm confused. Why does he seem so mad, and why is it directed at me? "Thank God! I was so worried! I'm so glad you—"

"Don't!" he holds up a hand to stall me. "Don't come any closer."

I take a step back in surprise. "Why? What are you..."

"It was you!" Thad points at me.

My mind is blank. "What was me?"

"You did this." He points to his head.

To my absolute horror, I start laughing. I don't know what's come over me, but it's the most ridiculous thing Thad has ever said to me. Until I look around the room and see that no one else is laughing. I spin around, meeting the eyes of each family member, and my laughter halts abruptly.

"You can't be serious." I look again.

Dad is looking at the ground. Melly looks confused and concerned, but at least she is meeting my eyes. Like she is searching for something, some answer in my actions. Casey is still biting her nails, and now she's so folded in on herself, her hair is practically covering her face. But Mom has me the most worried. She's staring right into my eyes. She's angry, and her fists are clenched to her sides.

"I am serious, Kelsey. It was you. You hit me with a shovel." Thad folds his hands over his chest.

"But I was here," I protest. "With all of you. Remember, we sat in the main room and discussed what to do before we all decided to go looking for Thad."

"You did take a very long shower," Melly offers up. But her eyes still convey her doubt.

"And? What do you think—that I left the shower running while I went out the two-story window, grabbed a shovel, ran to catch up with Thad, hit him in the head, climbed back up the two stories, and then came down-stairs? Do you know how much time that would take? Even if that was possible, why would I do that?"

Nobody answers me, but I can see from the way they haven't changed positions that my words have not changed anyone's mind. No one is rushing to my defense. How could they think this?

I turn and push back through them. I grab my coat from the coat rack and fling it around me. I'm almost at the front door when Dad's voice, loud, strong, and commanding, stops me in my tracks.

"Kelsey Kristine, you stop right there."

I resist the urge to put my hands in the air. But his voice is so authoritative, in a way I rarely heard. Like a cop getting ready to read me my rights. Instead, I obey, slowly turn, and put my hands in my pockets.

I'm locked into a stare down with Dad as my fingers on my right hand feel the rough ridges of what I immediately identify as keys. But I didn't drive here, and the keys to my apartment are upstairs in my purse. I search my memory to figure out whose keys are in my pocket.

Then it hits me. The missing snowmobile keys! The ones that Thad accused me of taking the day we found Ellen dead. I don't remember pocketing them, but he was right. I do have the keys. I must have slipped them in here without thinking about it. But adrenaline floods into my body. My family already thinks I'm guilty. What would they think if they knew I had the keys?

"What have you done, Kelsey?" Dad asks me.

Sudden confusion fills me. I drop my voice to a whisper. "I don't know."

# THIRTY-ONE

KELSEY

**4 Days to Christmas**

The angry and confused faces of each of my family members all focus on me. I look back at them, frozen with my hands on the handle of the front door. I was in flight mode until my fingers found the keys in my pocket. My pulse picks up and my breath feels short.

"What do you mean, you don't know?" Dad asks, his voice dripping with accusation.

"I mean, I don't know why Thad said I did that." I motion toward the open door where I can see Thad lying in bed, his face turned toward us. I try to remain logical, but I'm rattled. When did I take the keys?

"You're not going anywhere, young lady," Mom's voice raises from where she stands.

"Fine." I let my hand fall from the door and my eyes flick to the clear path up the stairs. I make a beeline for them and run up. Now, I'm sitting on the floor in the corner of my room upstairs with the door open. I don't want to give my family any more ammunition or cause for speculation about my whereabouts. The light is off, and it's pitch-black, with a blackout curtain over the window. Suddenly, it feels like the walls are closing in on me.

My breath is short, and I gasp as if I have been holding it. The air in the room is getting shallow, like I'm stuck in a coffin, and the oxygen is running out. Like the coffin that will hold Ellen. If anyone ever comes to help us. If we live through this. Whatever *this* is.

I think about the snowmobile key I found in my coat pocket. I had been so sure I didn't have it. What else do I feel sure about that isn't correct? My breath is coming in short, quick bursts now. My heart is accelerating. I feel a sweat break out over my back. For minutes, I am immobilized. Sitting perfectly still. Irrationally, I feel like if I move, something bad will happen. Like the bad things that have been happening all along.

I take a slow deep breath. It feels good, so I take another one. I'm starting to calm down. I'm self-regulating. I can give myself grace. So what if I palmed the keys to the snowmobile? It's not like I emptied the gas. I wouldn't even know how to cut the gas line. But people accidentally steal keys all the time.

Then I hear a beep. What was that? Maybe I imagined it. I wait for a minute. But I hear it again. A tiny, almost imperceptible *beep*. I lean forward and get on my knees and crawl in the direction I think I hear it. Then I stop and listen until it happens again. I'm at the edge of my bed.

When the beep sounds again, I place my hand under my mattress and gasp when my probing fingers find a rectangular case. I know before I bring it out that it's a cell phone. I put my finger on the front of it, highlighting the lock screen. Of course I don't have the password. It's not my phone. I can see several missed calls and texts waiting to be read. I can see the unread text from Thad. The phone calls are from Mom. And the picture behind all the activity is of Ellen and Mom snuggled close, cheek to cheek, with huge grins on their faces.

"Oh my God!" I whisper as I drop the phone on the ground and crawl backward, staring at it from afar. It's Ellen's phone. I have Ellen's phone shoved between the mattresses in my room. But I have no recollection of how it got there. Nor do I know how long it's been there. I have a sneaking suspicion that it will match the amount of time Ellen has been dead.

I am horrified and staring at the phone as if it's a living thing that somehow walked into my room after my sister died. But that's not the case. I just have no other logical explanation, and I know my family will jump to the wrong conclusions. Conclusions I have no way to prove are false.

But as I sit looking at the still-lit-up screen in my dark room, something else occurs to me. This phone has service. Maybe it's a weird fluke, but I need to utilize this before the service goes away.

I scramble back to the phone and push 9-1-1. I put the phone up to my ear.

"Nine one one, what's your emergency?" the voice responds.

"You actually answered." Relieved tears flood my eyes.

"My sister was found dead. My brother was attacked and needs medical attention. Our address is—"

There's a click sound, and the call drops. I know it before I can get any other words out.

"No!" I gasp. I look at the phone screen. There are no bars of service. I move to the right and to the left, but it doesn't help. No bars show up on the screen. I wedge the phone back under the mattress and pull it back out but it's no use. I stand and walk around the room, staring at the display. Nothing. Not only does it not show any bars in the corner, the screen says, *No Service.*

Then I have a horrible realization. I just used Ellen's phone to call 9-1-1. They will have her number. The phone records will show that a call was placed on Ellen's phone after her time of death.

My family already thinks I'm guilty. They want to pin Ellen's murder on me, and with Thad downstairs telling them that I hit him in the head with a shovel, I'm as good as convicted.

How will I be able to prove that I had nothing to do with Ellen's death when the evidence is starting to stack up against me? Keys, phone, an eyewitness who puts me at the scene of his attack. I've watched crime fiction and read legal thrillers. My next phone call, should I get service, might need to be to a lawyer. Because I'm starting to look mighty guilty here.

# THIRTY-TWO

KELSEY

**3 Days to Christmas**

It is after midnight when I finally regain my wits and decide to leave my room. I assume my family is asleep, and I'm trying to avoid them. I'm not thinking about the overnight watch we put in place. I just know I've managed to avoid their judgmental looks and potentially snarky questions for the entire day. But now, I'm hungry, and I can't sit in my dark room another minute.

I quietly creep to the stairs on stocking feet. My warm fuzzy socks are the only thing making me feel comfortable right now. My skin is crawling. I feel like I'm doing something wrong. But I'm not. I have to remind myself of that.

My family did not put me in my room as a jail all day. I did. I chose to be there. Away from their prying eyes.

I make it to the kitchen and find a night-light plugged into the wall. I flip the switch and am relieved when it gives me just enough light to illuminate the kitchen but not enough to wake a house.

I turn and reach for the refrigerator when movement catches the corner of my eye. I turn and a startled squeak pops out of my mouth.

Thad is sitting at the dining room table, and he is staring at me with anger and something else. Confusion. I still, not moving as we stare at each other.

Finally, unable to take the loaded silence, I crack. "You're out of bed. Should you be—"

"Cut the crap, Kelsey," Thad interrupts me. "Why did you do it? Why did you hit me? What if I hadn't woken up? Is that what you intended?" His arms are crossed in front of him leaning on the table, like he's interrogating a suspect. And I realize, he is. I notice how strong his biceps are and how tightly coiled his arms are. Thad isn't afraid of me. He's angry and ready to defend himself if he needs to.

I sink down to the chair opposite him. I decide to tread lightly. I've seen Thad angry more than once, mostly when we were younger, and it's a sight to behold. I don't want to set him off by calling him crazy. Instead, my therapist training kicks in, shocking even me.

"Tell me why you think it was me," I say quietly.

Thad's eyes widen in a flare of disbelief, and his jaw clenches. "Because I saw you. It's not like someone just smacked me from behind, and I never saw a face, then blacked out. I saw you."

"Okay, tell me more." I know my tone is everything here. If I'm not careful, I will come off as placating.

"Is this some kind of joke?" Thad says sharply, then he looks around, seeming to realize that the house is quiet with sleeping people. He lowers his voice. "I was walking through the snow, taking the same path we took on the snowmobile, when I heard something behind me. And there you were."

"Okay, what was I doing?" I keep my tone relaxed to encourage him to keep talking.

"You were running after me. Sort of shuffle running. You were carrying a shovel," Thad explains.

"I was running through the snow with a shovel?" I try to keep my voice neutral, but something about this image strikes me as delusional. I don't run anywhere, even on dry days. Why would I run in the snow? What is Thad up to?

Color floods Thad's face. He must realize how ridiculous it sounds as well. "I know what I saw, Kelsey. I don't know why you did what you did. That's why I'm asking you."

I maintain eye contact and nod. "Okay, so you see me come running up with a shovel in my hand and what... I just swung it at you and hit your head?"

"No, Jesus. What is this conversation?" Thad scrubs his hand down his face. "I said *hi*. You asked what I was doing, and I explained that I was going to walk a bit farther to get bars of service. I turned back around to keep walking and bam. That's the last thing I remember."

"Just, bam? Just like that, I hit you? With no provocation or explanation?" I lean forward now as if I'm interrogating him, forgetting all my counselor training. I'm utterly baffled.

"Yeah, Kelsey," Thad snaps.

"See, I don't know what to say to all this because I never left the house until we all decided you were gone too long and went looking for you. We split up, and Casey and I were a group. We were the ones who found you—"

"Convenient, wouldn't you say?" Thad interrupts. "You found Ellen, too."

"That doesn't mean anything," I hold my hands up in gentle protest. "I was just telling you that I have an alibi for every minute you were gone and after we found you and brought you back."

Thad is shaking his head. "It's just like the frying pan incident."

I stare at Thad in disbelief. "The frying pan..." My mind wanders to when we were young. I'm having a hard time remembering.

"It was right after I arrived with this new family. You hit me in the back of the head with a frying pan, in the exact spot you hit me with the shovel." Thad's hand circles his head like a halo.

"I didn't hit you with a shovel!" I blurt in frustration, forgetting my efforts to remain calm. But then the frying pan incident comes flooding back to me with startling clarity. It was right after Thad joined the family. Not that I was allowed to refer to him as *new*. According to my mom, Thad had always been with us, and we weren't allowed to talk about any past days when he wasn't. It was an odd form of gaslighting. Like Mom was trying to convince us we'd always existed together in one happy family. Like all our trauma had been erased.

Thad had quite the temper back then. We were probably eight and nine years old. I had been coloring at the table, minding my own business, when Thad snatched the marker I'd been using and took off running.

Of course, I went after him. But somehow, even though

he was in the wrong and had started it, he turned on me. He was suddenly screaming in my face and pushing me. He told me I was a brat and wouldn't share with him. He said all he wanted to do was color with me, and I said *no*.

The feelings of fear came back to me sharp and clear. In that moment, I looked at Thad and thought about how much taller he was than me, even though he was younger. He pushed me again, and I turned and ran. He ran after me. He was so fast, and I could hear his breath behind me. He was gaining on me. Then I ran through the kitchen and grabbed a frying pan off the counter. Mom had set it out for dinner, but it wasn't hot or on the stove.

I ran through the kitchen to the utility room. But I was stuck. I had no way out of that room. So, I flattened myself to the wall beside the doorway and waited until Thad burst through the door. I thought he was going to kill me. I swung the frying pan hard and connected with the back of his head.

Thad crumpled, and there was blood everywhere. I started screaming. Mom came flying in and gasped. In her haste to stop the blood, she grabbed a towel and put it on Thad's head. When she looked at me, she was angry and frightened.

*What did you do?* she'd asked.

"I forgot about that," I whisper to Thad, feeling sudden shame.

"Yeah, it's pretty convenient how you forget bad things that happened when you were the one who instigated them," Thad spits out.

"What's that supposed to mean?" I feel shocked. Where is this coming from?

"You know what?" Thad says. "This is pointless. I'm

going to bed. And I'm locking my door." He gets up and leaves.

I'm left alone in the kitchen feeling helpless and full of bad memories and false accusations. I never claimed to be perfect. But what am I, exactly?

# THIRTY-THREE

KELSEY

**3 Days to Christmas**

I do not get food. After my confrontation with Thad, I cannot eat. In fact, my stomach is roiling, twisting, and turning in a way that makes me wonder if I will keep down what little I do have in my stomach. I have no doubt that if I try to open Thad's bedroom door right now, I'll find it locked. Instead, I am back in my own bedroom, but I cannot sleep. I pace around in the dark.

Why did I not remember the frying pan incident? Until Thad mentioned it, I had no recollection of it. What else have I forgotten from my childhood? I try to put myself back in that moment to feel what I felt. No prominent emotion stands out to me. With Thad angrily chasing me, I can imagine feeling helpless and afraid. Adult me understands how the whole situation escalated. What I find interesting is why I grabbed a weapon to defend myself at that age.

I sigh. Unfortunately, the answer lies in my traumatic past. The point when I woke up and found Kammy with her throat slit next to me. I subconsciously trace my own light scar across my neck. Twins share everything, and I hate that we shared this mark of violence. Sometimes it felt like I had absorbed her into my being. Like she had never existed, and it had been me, alone in that room all along.

I adamantly shook my head. *No!* I would not erase Kammy from existence. That was the kind of crazy that my adopted mom had tried to instill in us. She should have had us in counseling as we transitioned into the new home. Instead, she pretended that nothing bad had ever happened —to any of us. That what had happened prior to our place in the Caper household had ceased to exist. We only existed as a member of the Caper family. Nothing else was acceptable.

But I had clung to the trauma and the loss of my twin sister, holding her close to me, like a guilty secret. All the while, refusing to walk through the steps of healing to let her go as I progressed through my degree program. My own counselor had only heard the story in passing, and when I'd robotically explained what had happened, I told her that I wasn't willing to talk about it. It was my past, and it needed to remain there.

A gasp pushes past my lips, and I flip on a night-light. Urgently, I begin to dig through my suitcase for my journal. What I wouldn't give for my DSM-5, but it is too big to travel with me. I will have to rely on notes I took in class. In fact, my whole dissertation was on family dysfunction with an emphasis on coping mechanisms. I fixated on dissociative illnesses such as dissociative identity disorder, dissociative amnesia (as well as dissociative fugue), and depersonalization or derealization disorder.

I yank my notebook free of the heavy sweaters and jeans resting on top of it and frantically start flipping through until I find the generalized definition of dissociative illness. My finger follows as my eyes read the words. Then, I read them again.

My lips murmur aloud. "Dissociative disorders include difficulties with memory, identity, emotion, perception, behavior, and sense of self." I stop reading and stare up at the wall. We had been warned in the program about self-diagnosis. Patients often come into initial appointments with some knowledge of a mental illness they have self-diagnosed after extensively Googling their symptoms. This can be dangerous and lead to misdiagnosis and pushy behavior with therapists who try to back them out of that box, start at the beginning, and come to a decision about if the patient even has an illness in the first place.

And here I am, doing the exact same thing. Was I really attempting to diagnose myself of some illness? *Maybe*, I reasoned with myself, *I have the education and knowledge to do so successfully.*

But then my professor's voice objects to my thoughts. *You may have the book knowledge, but at the point that you graduate, you don't have the hands-on field experience. That's why you will be under supervision until you achieve the necessary hours to fully function on your own as a therapist.*

I have a long way to go. But I have to wonder if all this forward thinking, degree-seeking has been a way to deflect my own dysfunction. I sit with that for minutes, staring off into the distance, but seeing nothing.

There's one thing I know for sure. I have never given the time and energy necessary to address and heal from my past. My dreams and nightmares have been my body's attempts to uncover what I've kept hidden. A way to protect myself. Repression, both conscious and subconscious, is an effective coping mechanism that has helped me live a functional life. Hasn't it been?

I throw my notebook on the floor and turn off my night-light. I curl up in a little ball on the floor, feeling those emotions from childhood. Fear, confusion, and doubt flood into me, paralyzing me. The question playing on repeat in my mind keeps me from sleeping.

What if I haven't been functioning at all? I think about the keys, the cell phone, the behavior Thad described that matched my reaction as a child. What if I simply can't recall my actions? What if my mind's attempt to protect me has become deadly to those around me?

# THIRTY-FOUR

KELSEY

**3 Days to Christmas**

I wake with a start. Someone is watching me. The daylight creeping into my room through the crack in the curtains is casting long shadows. My heart is beating fast, and my eyes scan the room. The feeling of eyes on me are piercing.

Then, I see her. I gasp as my eyes take in her outline. She turns her back on me and opens the closet door. She wordlessly stands there, peering in.

"Mom?" I whisper. Despite how much her presence jolts me, I don't want to alarm her in case she's sleepwalking.

She turns. Her hair is a mess, like she just woke up. Her

shoulders are sloped, more than normal, making her look small and vulnerable in her flannel pajama set.

Her eyes fall on me, dull and unfocused. She smiles lightly.

"Oh, Kelsey." Her voice is a quiet singsong. "I'm looking for Ellen. Have you seen her?"

Immediate tears spring to my eyes at the mention of the sister who will never come home.

"No, Mom. She's—"

"Ellen loves to play hide-n-seek." Mom laughs softly before dropping to her knees and peering under my bed.

My breath catches in my chest. I know she's having an episode, but I don't want to be the one to bring her to the present by reopening the wound of Ellen's death.

"Ellen, where are you?" Mom calls quietly. She gets back on her feet.

"She's not here, Mom," I say when her expectant eyes fall on mine.

"Where is she?" Now she sounds impatient, her frustration showing.

"She's gone," I whisper. Tears fall down my face as I feel the pain of that truth all over again.

"There you are." Dad's jovial voice interrupts her reaction. "Come downstairs, Marney. Coffee's ready."

"But Ellen—" she protests.

"I know. We'll find her," he says, shuffling Mom out of the room. He pokes his head back in, noting my wide eyes over his blatant lie.

"It's better this way," he explains. "They say to let her mind stay in the past instead of startling her back to the present." Then he leaves.

I pull the covers over my head, letting my tears fall over Ellen and over the irony that Mom is happier in the past than she is in the here and now. I cry myself back to sleep.

I wake up on the floor of my bedroom. Light streams in from where I had moved the blackout curtains to look outside the night before.

I had never considered snow to be bleak and deadly until this vacation. As I stand and attempt to stretch out the sore muscles and kink in my neck, I gaze out the window. The snow is still falling in sheets, and it is even deeper than I thought possible. We're not getting out of here any time soon. I try not to think about Brax's attempt to do so. It has been a day, and no help has come. I can only surmise what that means.

When I get out of the shower, I notice something is happening downstairs. There are loud exclamations. I can hear Thad's voice boom louder than anyone else. He's shouting commands. There are sounds of shuffling and footsteps running back and forth. It sounds like utter chaos has exploded on the first floor.

Then the lights go out. A terse silence follows. The house is cast into pitch blackness, save that little light streaming into my room. I wrench the curtains the rest of the way open.

My heart rate accelerates as I throw on a pair of jeans and a sweatshirt. I ignore my wet hair that hangs in tangles around my face and open the bedroom door. The smell of smoke immediately fills my nose, and the temperature out here is significantly warmer than my bedroom. I gasp at how thick the air feels. I cough as the fumes seem to coat my throat. I rush down the stairs.

"Fire!" Mom yells as she rushes past with a bucket of water. She's moving as fast as she can without spilling a drop of it on the carpet. Then Casey runs by with baking soda. She's so focused on her task, she doesn't seem to see me.

For half a second, I freeze. I process the scene. Did they turn off the power to contain the fire, or did the fire take out the electricity? My eyes search the house to find the source of the commotion. Then I see it. There's a lick of flame crawling up the wall. The back door is open, and I can see Thad standing out in the snow, like he's directing traffic. *This is Thad after a brain injury?* But then, I read that adrenaline can make people do unimaginable things.

"No water!" he barks. "It's electrical. We need blankets."

His words shake me out of my stupor. I sprint for the linen closet, open the door, and reach in. I have an armful of blankets, sheets, and towels before Casey even makes it inside the house.

I drop the load in the snow at the feet of a surprised looking Thad. "Shit, Kelsey. We didn't even—"

"Don't worry about it," I cut him off. Was he going to apologize for not waking me up or letting me know about the fire? I can't think about that right now. None of that matters until we get this under control. "Listen, the fire on the inside is spreading up the wall. We need someone working on that."

"No!" he snaps. "None of you are trained to put out a fire." He picks up several blankets and takes them inside.

I ignore his command, grab my own blankets, and mimic his actions. Before I can walk back into the house, a hand stops me. It's my dad. "Kelsey, Thad's a firefighter. This is what he does. You need to leave this to him."

I shake off his hand. "He has a brain injury. Plus, it's moving too fast." I rush back into the house and gasp at the heat inside and the magnitude of the flame. Dad was right. I'm not trained for this.

Thad is attempting to tamp down the flame with blankets. I quickly work beside him. I can surmise he is attempting to smother the flame. I'm not sure why we shouldn't use water, but somewhere I heard that dealing with an electrical fire had a different process.

"You shouldn't be in here!" Thad shouts over the now dull crackle of the fire.

"You're in here," I shoot back, my eyes never leaving the wall. I would not have thought a blanket over a fire would ever work, but the flames are slowly subsiding.

Thad doesn't respond.

Relief floods through me as the flame subsides to a small light at the base of the wall. Casey chooses that moment to come in with more blankets. She jumps in, copying our actions.

"There's still fire on the other side," she reports.

Our side of the wall is smoldering, so Thad, Casey, and I run back outside just in time to catch Mom mid-throw with a bucket of water.

"No!" Thad shouts, but it is too late.

Water douses the flame and soaks the wood from the wall. Thad puts a hand out and shoves us all back protectively. I have no idea what happens when water is thrown on an electrical fire. I half expect sparks to shoot back at us and electrocute us. As I glanced at Thad, I have a feeling he thought the same thing. But the result is the opposite.

The flame diminishes. Then it goes out completely. In its place is a blackened wall of the cabin, drenched and already icing over. No one speaks for minutes as we stand in the snow, none of us realizing that we are not dressed for the elements. We are freezing out here.

That's when I feel an arm circle my shoulder. I look to find Melly with sorrow in her eyes. "I'm sorry we didn't get you up. We all just sort of reacted."

Her words sting, but not because they are caring and kind. I am trying not to focus on how they all forgot me in the wake of a crisis. The grown up me understands completely, that as an adult, I am responsible for myself. It is not their job to save me. Only I can save myself. But the child in me feels like crying. How quickly I slipped from their thoughts.

It feels like abandonment, and it is an irrational reaction. Like the night my twin sister was killed in the bed right next to me. She didn't intentionally abandon me, but the way she was ripped out of my life was so sudden and jarring.

"It wasn't electrical," Thad murmurs, breaking the stillness. His voice sounds like he's in shock.

"What?" I turn to look at him.

Thad is staring at the smoke damaged wall as if in a daze. "I thought the fire was electrical—due to faulty old wiring. When Mom doused the fire with water, it didn't react the way an electrical fire would have. It put the fire out."

"If it wasn't electrical, how did it start?" I ask.

All eyes fall on Thad now.

Thad gazes back at me. "Somebody started it."

I gasp and hear my family around me do the same. Then I notice the way Thad is looking at me very pointedly. He can't mean...

I peel my eyes from Thad and glance at Mom, Dad, Casey, and Melly. They all hold some variation of doubt and confusion as they all look back at me. My heart sinks in my chest.

"You have got to be kidding!" I exclaim. The cold suddenly rushes in, and I feel, rather than see, that my wet hair has become icicles on my head. I pluck at an icy strand of hair. "I was in the shower. You guys are the ones who left me upstairs to burn alive!"

My statement is dramatic, I will admit to that, but I will not admit to arson. I wasn't anywhere near this part of the house. I've been in my room for hours.

Right?

# THIRTY-FIVE

THAD

**3 Days to Christmas**

Once the family drifts back inside, I hear them making preparations to clean up the damage. Someone suggests opening the front door to air out the smoke. It's a good idea, but all of that fades to background noise. Not that I would admit it to them, but my head is a little fuzzy, and I feel off-kilter, dizzy. That's what I get for trying to fight a fire post head injury. But I had no choice. I should go in and rest.

First though, I have to check the structure to make sure it's sound. The last thing we need is to have an outer wall collapse on us. I take several steps backward in the snow and assess the scorch mark patterns. I look for cracks in the outer wall and in the foundation. I view the blackened surfaces. Then I check to see if the wall of the house or the window are leaning in any way. I look for damaged electrical or gas lines. While there's clear fire damage and color disfiguration, the house doesn't appear unsafe. When I'm satisfied, I go inside and run through the same mental checklist. But I know I'm forgetting some things. My head is pulsing.

When I enter, I scan my family. They're sitting at the dining room table. It's quiet as they each cling to big coffee mugs in front of them. They are bundled in winter wear to withstand the icy cold wind that is whipping inside. It's cold, but it's effective in airing out the smoke fumes. I don't warn Mom and Dad that the furniture will likely need to be replaced. There's no real way to clean couches and love seats to fully erase the smoke smell.

I knock on places where I think there are studs in the wall and find everything soundly holding the wall up. I scan the house to make sure there are no leftover embers anywhere that can ignite a new flame. I walk around the floor and bounce on the stairs in the staircase. I look at the ceiling and notice it's holding up with no sagging. I think through everything I can remember until I am convinced the fire was contained on this one wall, and we extinguished it fast enough to contain it.

But none of that explains the source of the fire.

"How did this fire get set?" It's my job to analyze fire sources for insurance claims. When we suspect arson, we hand it over to law enforcement to figure out who started it. I grind my teeth thinking about my sister's dead body lying at the woodshed that we have yet to move. I think about my attack. Now, the attack was on my entire family. But there is no way to call the police.

I was livid when I woke to find that Brax had taken the vehicle. Our one potential way out of this nightmare of a holiday, and Brax has stolen it. I want to believe the best of Brax, that he will bring back help, but he's a selfish prick. I didn't like him when he and Casey met, my opinion never changed, and his actions earlier this week reinforce that. What kind of a man hits on another man's wife in front of him, with his own partner sitting a chair away? His behavior on this vacation has cemented my dislike for him.

I shake my head over the inner turmoil. But what supersedes all of that is my sister, Kelsey. She acts so innocent. She even helped fight the fire. What kind of game is she playing? When I was out searching for cell service, I was surprised when she came running up to me. She was dragging a shovel behind her, eliminating her footprints as she moved.

"Kelsey, I've got this. Only one of us needs to call for help. I told you to stay in the house," I told her. Then I made the mistake of turning my back on her. The shock of the pain as I went down caught me so off guard, I didn't think to fight back. It was Kelsey. I trusted her. I fell face first and tried to move, to get back up. I think I must have gotten to my knees before I felt a second hit. I blacked out until I woke up to Melly's beautiful face hovering over mine.

For that reason, I think it was Kelsey who somehow started the fire. I have no idea how she could have gotten down here and set it without one of us seeing her, but I didn't know she would attack me either.

I get real close to the wall and bend to investigate a smell. I don't know how I missed it in all the chaos, but I did. It's sharp, tangy, and potent. I lower myself to the foundation, and the smell becomes sharper. I follow it outside with my nose. It's gasoline. I turn the corner.

Someone doused one side of the house at the base, where the ground is dry with no snow on account of the roof overhang. I look around for a lighter or a match, though I suppose whoever did this would not be stupid enough to leave behind that evidence. But then I freeze. There's a match laying on the ground right in plain sight. I decide not to mess with the evidence at a crime scene.

I stand and gauge the distance between here and the woodshed. It isn't far. I know if I go over there, I will find that the gasoline can Dad keeps on hand for the snowmobile will be empty.

I can only determine this is Kelsey, too. I just can't figure out why, and I'm not sure what to do about it. I go back inside. My family looks at me expectantly. I'm having a hard time articulating my suspicions. They have a right to know, don't they?

My eyes fall on each of them, locking with Kelsey's. Her hands are in the pockets of her coat. She brings them out quickly and holds them up like she's surrendering. But as her hands comes out, a key loudly clatters to the floor. My eyes catch the movement, and I am instantly moving. There's a plastic key chain with the word *Montana* on it and the outline of the mountains. It's faded to a muted yellow with age. I know with certainty that this is the key to the snowmobile. Kelsey has had it in her pocket all along.

I scoop it up and whirl to her. "What the hell is this, Kelsey?"

Her face turns white. She opens her mouth to speak but shuts it. "I—"

"It's the key to the snowmobile." I hold it up and show my family.

There's a collective gasp in the room.

"I don't know how it got there," Kelsey sputters.

"Hmm," I answer. I address the room. "Someone set the fire intentionally."

There's another gasp.

"We can't get law enforcement up the mountain for help, but there is a way to contain what's happening here." I use my most authoritative voice.

"How?" Dad asks.

The rest of the family stares mutely.

I point at Kelsey. "House arrest."

"What?" Casey breathes.

"I did not do any of this..." Kelsey tries weakly to defend herself. Even she doesn't look convinced.

"We can't take that chance." I'm not giving room for any argument. "Let's go."

No one says a word as I grab Kelsey by the arm and haul her to her feet. I take her to her room with strong admonishing not to leave. Then I go downstairs to find tools. I'm going to turn the lock to face outward. Kelsey will not be able to do any more damage to the family this Christmas.

When I come back through the living room carrying a screwdriver, Dad stops me.

"Son, you can't lock her in there. It's not right."

I clench my fists and grit my teeth. "If we have her locked up and nothing else happens, we'll have our answer."

"Will we?" he challenges.

As I stare at him, I know he's right. We can't prove anything. Except that she hit me. In a court of law, that would be assault and battery. We wouldn't be able to prove attempted murder.

"Fine!" I say. "But she's not leaving that room without a pair of eyes on her at all times!"

# THIRTY-SIX

KELSEY

**3 Days to Christmas**

In the aftermath of the fire, I have been placed on house arrest. Unconstitutionally, I might add. So much for a trial. Thad went back downstairs after explicitly telling me not to go anywhere. I wouldn't have anyway. The solace of my room offers me the chance to leave behind the accusing stares of my family. I'm not alone here for long. I hear loud footsteps on the stairs and what I perceive are mean, blaming steps coming closer with every *thump, thump, thump*. I assume Thad has returned.

I fling open my bedroom door to find myself face-to-face with Casey.

Casey's normally brown eyes are dark with anger and another emotion—fear, perhaps? "What the hell, Kels!"

I take a step back in surprise. Of all of us, Casey's style is to address problems with sarcastic jokes instead of direct confrontation. In fact, I can't think of a time I've ever seen her come at me. But there's nothing sarcastic in her gaze now.

"What do you mean?" I retreat further back into the sanctuary that has become my room.

"I mean, our house just caught on fire, and you look really guilty—"

"After I helped put it out?" I protest. I'm on the defense, and with every word, I take a step backward, trying to put distance between me and my sister. Casey keeps advancing, attempting to step into my personal space. I take a deep breath to offset the one I've been holding. "I can't take the way you all keep looking at me. Like I'm some kind of wild animal you need to study to understand."

"God, I'm trying so hard to give you the benefit of the doubt, but your actions are so suspicious!" Casey takes another step closer. I can see the whites of her eyes around her dark angry irises.

My breath catches in my chest, and my head feels light. I don't know how to ward her off. I can't prove my innocence here. Every time I try, I sound lame and suspicious. Even to my own ears.

"I was in the shower when the fire started. I can't even understand how you all—"

Casey pokes a finger to my chest. "That was your excuse last time, too."

"Because it's true!" I choke out. This step backward puts my back against the wall. It feels like they are closing in around me. "Why doesn't anyone believe me? Can't you hear the shower from downstairs?"

Casey doesn't answer. Inexplicably, she turns and stalks to the window and stares out like she's considering how I might make my getaway.

I take the moment to close my eyes and take a deep breath in and out. Casey hums like she's mystified.

"What are you doing?" Her sharp voice is in front of me.

I really wish she would give me space. I slowly open my eyes. "I need you to back up."

"What?"

"I can't breathe. That doesn't mean I'm guilty of anything. I'm just feeling extremely claustrophobic right now, and you are in my personal space, which is not helping me." I learned about boundaries in my program. Why is it so hard to practice them now?

"Oh, I'm sorry." Casey's sarcastic edge is back. "Am I crowding you?"

I nod weakly.

Casey steps forward again. "Does this make you nervous?"

"Yes. Please give me space."

Casey ignores my request. "Are you glad Ellen is dead?"

I snap. Something inside me rips, and the anger I keep buried deep inside unleashes. My hand pulls back, and my palm connects with Casey's face in one satisfying movement. The sharp slap against skin reverberates in the sudden stillness of the room. It's deathly quiet.

Before Casey puts a hand to her face, I see the angry red fingermarks put there by my own hand. Casey's eyes are wide and unblinking. My mouth is stuck, hanging open. We are both frozen.

All I can think is, *I've never been violent before.* I've never struck another person in my life. Why did I hit her?

"I'm sorry—"

"How could you—"

We both speak at the same time, then stop. Finally, Casey takes a step back. I suppose I should be grateful she's not advancing to retaliate. Lord knows she would have when we were kids. But then, I remember the simple fact that might be holding her in place.

Casey is pregnant. She can't risk losing the baby in some thug brawl with her sister. Her sister whom she always loved and defended. Until now.

"You were in my space, and I warned you." I might as well have singsonged the words *I warned you.* I cross my arms over my chest. "And I'm so tired of being accused." My voice sounds petulant, like I'm ten. I'm still standing with my back against the wall, only now, the wall feels comforting. A surface that is holding my body upright.

"I don't even know who you are anymore." As Casey takes another step backward, I feel an odd sense of panic. *No!* I don't want to lose my sister. I can't stand the thought of her turning her back on me. Her opinion of me is suddenly the most important thing in my life.

"Casey, please." I push off the wall and reach for her.

Casey takes two steps back rapidly and shakes her head. "Don't come any closer. We're done. You and me. We're done."

"No!" I cry out and chase her as she exits my bedroom.

I stare at the door long after she's gone. *What is happening to me?* This isn't me. I crumple to the floor and cry, feeling like someone has just severed an appendage.

# THIRTY-SEVEN

KELSEY

**3 Days to Christmas**

A pounding headache alerts me that I haven't eaten yet, but it takes me half a day to get up the courage to sneak downstairs. As I tiptoe to the banister and look over, I see my entire family sitting in the living room in various positions of despair.

Thad and Melly are clinging to each other. Melly's eyes are closed, and Thad is staring suspiciously at the black fire-damaged wall. Casey is flipping her phone around, pausing every once in a while to look at the screen as if the Wi-Fi will magically start working. I wonder if she's worrying about Brax. Mom and Dad are sitting on recliners on opposite sides of the living room. Mom is looking out the window at the snow, and Dad is pretending to work a crossword puzzle, but I can see from my place on the landing that the page is untouched.

Though an outsider might consider my family the picture of nonchalance right now, I know what lurks under the surface. No part of me wants to go down there. But I won't stay in my room forever. They can't prove any of this was me. I'm innocent until proven otherwise.

Despite my inner determination, I quake outwardly. I can't make myself go down there. I don't care how hungry I am. They are all angry at me. They have made up their minds, and no matter what I tell them, it won't change anything.

*They hate you.* The thought materializes, and once it takes root, I begin to believe it. *You've always been the outsider.* That is true. I have not ever fit in. Here or anywhere in my life. *You assaulted your sister.* What they think about me now is somewhat true.

I try to tell myself I don't care what they think. But it is a lie. What my family thinks of me is everything. I've always prided myself on my image and how I present the facts. Maybe those are just stories I tell myself and impose on others. If people out there think I have my life together, then that means I do. I'm a good leader. I'm reliable, resourceful, and self-sufficient. I'm disciplined, *damn it.* Only, what I did to Casey—the way I hauled off and hit her across the face—lacks all self-control.

What's that expression? Be careful pointing the finger because you'll find three fingers pointing back at you. Well, downstairs there awaits a room full of family, the people who should be closest to me in my life, pointing the blame at me.

I have never felt more alone. My vision blurs a bit. My

body sways as dizziness hits me. I reach for the wall behind me and slump against it. I slowly slide my body down until my bottom hits the wood floor with a soft thud. Sweat forms on my temples. I take in big gulps of air, but I can't seem to catch my breath.

What if bad things just happen when I'm in the room? Like when my sister was murdered in the bed next to me, and I was unable to stop it. I wasn't able to stop Ellen's murder either. Or Thad's head injury. And I certainly didn't prevent the fire from happening. But something is going on here. If I were an aware, healthy person, maybe I would stop to consider that the fault belongs to me.

I think back to my dissertation notes. Dissociative amnesia is the inability to remember traumatic situations. Have I been blocking out my trauma since I was five years old? If so, all of this would be the manifestation of that single incident that changed my life forever.

How damaged am I really?

# THIRTY-EIGHT

## KELSEY

**3 Days to Christmas**

"Kelsey?"

My name travels to me through a thick fog and echoes like I am in a tunnel. Which is it? Am I in a fog or in a tunnel? A foggy tunnel? My body shakes suddenly. Okay, I'm in a foggy tunnel during an earthquake.

My eyelids flutter, and I see the faces of my family, all peering down at me with concern. It's enough to make me feel claustrophobic again. I put a hand up to push them back but manage to connect with no one.

"She's awake!" Thad's says, and he sounds... relieved.

"Back up, everyone. Give her some space." Melly kneels down at my side and puts a cold hand on my forehead.

"That feels nice. What happened?" I sift back through what I last remember. Watching my family downstairs pretending to be okay, when, clearly, they were not. But what is more pressing is how not okay I am.

"Casey found you passed out in the hallway up here." Melly continues patting my face. Then she puts two fingers to the pulse at my throat. I flinch a little because even though my scar is not deep, it's still a little sensitive.

I lick my lips. "I passed out?"

"Unless you decided to sleep in the hallway..." Casey quips.

My eyes snap to hers. She doesn't sound angry. She should be. I search her face for a sign of the hand print I put there earlier. There is nothing.

"Heart rate seems normal." Melly gently pulls down an eyelid. Then she does the same thing on the other side. "When is the last time you ate?"

"Umm..." I don't remember.

"I bet that's it. You didn't eat breakfast before the fire. You've been up here all day. Your body needs fuel, Kelsey. Let's get you up." Melly stands and offers a hand.

I take it and stand up. I feel relieved. Maybe my family is not angry at me anymore. Maybe everything will be okay. I walk downstairs and sit at the table while Mom fixes me a sandwich.

I consume the food and appreciatively drink the coffee she puts in front of me. I feel better until I hear the loud exclamation.

"What the hell is this?" Dad is coming out of my room and peering suspiciously at something in his hand.

I look up, watching him walk down the stairs. Then I notice he's holding a cell phone. From where I sit, I can see the screen lit up with a picture of Ellen and Mom on the screen. *Oh no!* I stare at it in horror. I thought I put that back under the mattress. Everyone is now looking at Ellen's phone.

Dad stops in front of me. He doesn't have to say anything. His eyes tell me everything he's thinking.

"It's a cell phone," Casey states the obvious. "What's the big deal?"

"It's Ellen's cell phone." Dad flashes it around the family, holding it like it's hot, and it will burn him.

There is a collective gasp from my entire family, and they all swivel to me, faces red, eyes piercing, arms crossed. I look from face to face, but there are no allies here.

"Why do you have Ellen's phone in your room?" Dad's eyes flash between concern to fear.

I am thankful no one has a pitchfork or fire poker handy. They are waiting for an explanation, but I do not have one.

"I don't know how that got in my room." My voice is quiet, and the words sound lame in my own ears.

"That's it!" Thad stomps around the kitchen, and I hear him shuffle in the cabinet until he comes away with a clear, plastic bag. He holds the bag out to Dad, who drops the phone in there like it is evidence and throws it on the table.

"What are you, like a cop now?" Casey jokes half-heartedly, but she's biting her fingernails and avoiding eye contact with me.

Dad steps forward as the judge and jury. "We need to figure out what to do next. Kelsey, go to your room."

"Why?" I'm as surprised as everyone else by what comes out of my mouth. "No."

"No?" Mom swivels to me. "You will not disrespect your father like that."

"For heaven's sake, Mom," I explode. "I'm twenty-nine years old. If there's a solution here, I need to be a part of it."

"Not if you're the one creating the problem!" Thad pounds his hand against the table so loud, we all jump.

A trickle of fear crawls down my spine. If I can't convince my family I'm innocent, then maybe I'm not. I have no way out of this. Nothing I say or do will convince them of my innocence. I am quickly realizing I have no other choice here.

"Fine!"

Without another word, I stand and storm toward the staircase. I stomp up them, making as much racket as I can, and when I get to my room, I slam the door hard. The walls shake, and I feel some satisfaction over that. But as I crawl into my bed and pull the covers up over me, I can't help but feel how much I regressed in that moment.

Like I was five years old again.

Maybe that's where all of this started. In a pitch-black room where two twin beds sit side by side. When I got to live, simply because Kammy's bed was positioned closest to our door.

"I can't." A sudden sob erupts from me. It's the topic I have avoided in therapy. If I talk about what happened, it's only to mention it in passing. I won't stay there and rehash the memory of that night. I'm too afraid of what it will do to my mental state.

But as I lie here in the darkish room, with eyes squeezed tightly shut, comforter covering my whole body, it occurs to me that my mental state is already unraveling. There's no putting it back where it was. There's only moving forward. Which I can't do if I'm permanently stuck in the past reliving Kammy's final moments. If we're going to survive this horrible holiday, snowed in, in the middle of nowhere, with no communication to the outside world, I need to process the night my twin sister, Kammy, was murdered.

# THIRTY-NINE

## THAD

**3 Days to Christmas**

My family looks stricken as we still sit around the kitchen table, and I unfold the last vote. After Kelsey went to her room, a door at the top of the stairs we can clearly see from the open layout of the first floor, we decided to take a vote on whether to lock Kelsey in her room or not. We kept it anonymous, writing down *yes* or *no* on a small slip of paper.

I tally the final vote. "Majority rules. Kelsey will be placed on house arrest and locked in her room."

Casey looks worried. "But we'll bring her dinner and check on her from time to time."

I nod. "Of course."

Kelsey has access to a bathroom, and I grab a couple

water bottles in addition to my screwdriver and a few basic hand tools.

I knock lightly on Kelsey's door, taking it upon myself to give her the news. She wrenches the door open, and I notice she's been crying. I feel bad, but I shouldn't. She's guilty. Still, I hold out the water bottles as some sort of peace offering.

Kelsey takes them and sets them on her dresser. Then she folds her arms over her chest, taking in my tools.

"So that's it then? You are all going to keep me here like a criminal?" she asks, her power of observation strong.

"We voted, Kelsey. Majority rules. It wasn't my choice." I'm lying. This was my choice from the beginning.

She nods, looking resigned and sad.

I get to work on turning the door lock. "It didn't have to be this way—"

"Save it." She puts up one hand, goes to the window, and turns her back on me, gazing out.

So, I do. I finish the task and shut the door quietly. I lock it and wonder why I don't feel any better. Shouldn't I feel some peace or resolution? After all, my goal is to keep my family safe.

But what about Kelsey? She's my family, too.

# FORTY

CASEY

**3 Days to Christmas**

I can't sleep. The house is quiet. The dresser is pushed snugly up against the door. I'm safe. At least, I think I am. Except for my mind, which keeps spinning and looping around.

Though I'm shocked that Kelsey slapped me, I know I got in her space, and she reacted. That seems like my fault. It doesn't prove that she's behind any of this—Ellen, Thad, or the fire. In fact, it wouldn't make sense. Seeing her room setup convinced me there's no possible way she could have gotten in and out without us noticing. It convinces me that Kelsey is innocent. This makes my mind wander to one other person who might be guilty.

The possibility leaves me breathless. It's so terrible, I don't want to consider it, but I keep replaying Brax lying about his prison time, his reprehensible behavior with Melly, and the way he left me. It's more of a feeling than fact, but something is off. There's no way he would have done any of that unless...

Brax is guilty. I can't bring myself to believe he would hurt anyone. I just know he's lying. About what? I'm not sure—this time.

When I chose Brax as my life partner, I chose him for his ability to have fun and help me take my mind off the seriousness of life. I try to keep things light, but occasionally, my hidden darkness creeps in.

When I was three years old, I lost both of my parents in a horrific car accident. I was wrapped safely in a car seat and untouched—a survivor. I could have grown up acting like a victim, the sad girl with no parents. I didn't. Instead, I chose to focus on the positive–I had lived. As a result, I've always tried to really live my life. It's the reason I travel.

I didn't go into a profession that saves people from traumatic situations or cleans up the aftermath like my siblings did. Kelsey thinks she's the only one who has figured out that each of them chose jobs related to their past pain—enabling them to help people the way they were helped. I choose to commemorate loved ones on people's bodies. What better living memorial than a tattoo of a loved one's name or a portrait of their face, forever remembered as they were in their prime of life?

Though Brax and I are connected in a way I never had with anyone else, I know I'm codependent with him. I want to know the truth about my partner, I do. But I dread knowing. If Brax is lying to me, I fear I'll have to act and make changes that will leave me utterly alone. Being alone is what I fear the most in life.

Which is why I am staring at Brax's suitcase like it has grown a pair of wings and is about to fly away. I did a tattoo like that once. I take a deep breath, knowing once I open his suitcase and go through it, everything will change. It officially signifies I don't trust him.

I know he's been angry at my family for years. What I need to know now is if he's angry enough to hurt them. Brax was out of the room as long as Kelsey was the other day when Thad was hurt. Everyone was so focused on Kelsey, they weren't thinking about Brax. Only I was. If I'm truthful with myself, I sometimes obsess over him.

I roll my neck and shake my hands, letting my feet do a little jog in place before I unzip his luggage and let the suitcase fall open. I dive my hands in and pull out shirts, sweatshirts, jeans, and a pair of shoes. When the suitcase is empty, my eyes fall on its two zippered pockets.

A sense of denial clouds me with the deep dread in my soul. I don't want to unzip those pockets. Somehow, I know what I'll find—the truth.

I reach for the zipper closest to me and unzip it slowly. I tell myself it's because I know the zipper catches. Really, it's because I don't want to see what's inside.

As the pouch pops open, my breath hitches. The smell singes my nostrils. He has a bag of weed double bagged and rolled up. I wonder if that's why we traveled by train. We didn't have a bag check like we would have in TSA. A giggle pops out of me, breaking up the tension in the room that I've created. Brax must have thought he needed this to be around my family.

I pick up the bag, unroll it, and take a deep breath as I peek in. Relief fills me. Smoking is our past time, and Brax clearly brought enough for me. Although, I guess I shouldn't smoke with my diagnosis.

Still holding the baggie, my eyes fall on what's left in the luggage pocket. One lighter and a small matchbox. I reach for it, flip open the lid, and freeze. There's one match missing.

My mind fills in the blanks. Thad said the fire was started. Did he mentioned finding a match? I remember a snatch of conversation I had with Brax on the way here.

*"What are you going to do, make them apologize?"*

*"Yes."*

*"How?"*

*"I'll club them over the head."*

*"No, you won't."*

*"Fine, I'll set the house on fire."*

*"Stop it. Thad's a firefighter. He'd just put the blaze out."*

*"Fine."*

My mind wanders. Thad is a firefighter. Brax and Thad exchanged punches in the past few days. There's no love lost there. Was Brax trying to send a message that he could get past Thad's defenses? The fire happened after Brax left. What if he didn't really leave?

I drop the box of matches and bag like they burned me. I'm jumping to conclusions. My hands shake now as they move to unzip the second pocket in Brax's luggage.

I peer in, gasp, and jump back. It's a knife. A pocketknife with a serrated edge. It's big and malicious. Brax isn't violent. He doesn't own weapons. Yet, what I'm looking at proves that wrong. Maybe he thought there would be an emergency, and he would need it. But my gut is telling me that's not why he brought it.

I look around and locate a pair of leather snow gloves. I pull them on and rush back to the knife. Carefully, I open it.

It looks expensive and mean. This sharp weapon could do serious damage.

Something catches my eye as I turn over the blade. A small patch of rust adorns the tip and trickles half an inch down the edge. I bring it closer to my face, into my direct eyeline. Ice flushes into my veins.

That's not rust. It's blood.

# FORTY-ONE

## CASEY

**3 Days to Christmas**

My phone flashlight illuminates a spot on the ground. I'm outside in the dark scanning the side of the blackened house where the fire raged just this morning. It's hard to believe that was earlier today. The section of the ground closest to the house is dry, which makes it easy to see.

When I spot a single match lying on the ground, I freeze. There's no way to know if the match came from the matchbox upstairs in Brax's luggage. But the pieces are falling together in a way I can't deny any more.

"What do you think you're doing?"

"Shit!"

I whirl around and drop my phone in the snow. The

flashlight casts an eerie glow up into the night sky. In my haste to find the truth, I forgot that someone is lurking around trying to pick off my family one by one. But if that someone is Brax, I will be safe, right? The thought sends a chill through me.

I can see a large body standing beside me. I blink a few times and see Thad. Relief fills me until I see the anger in his eyes.

"Geez, Thad, you scared me!"

"I could say the same thing to you. What are you doing out here, Casey?" There's a steel edge in his voice, and I know I won't be able to pull off a lie. I point to the match on the ground. "Did you know that was there?"

Thad's confused look swings to where I'm pointing. He nods slowly. "I noticed it a few hours ago. Damning evidence for arson."

I sigh. "I have something to show you."

"Okay." Thad follows me back into the house and up to my room.

He stands in the doorframe as I show him the knife. His eyes widen when I flip open the match book to reveal one missing match.

"What if it's not Kelsey?" I whisper.

Thad's eyes dart to the room down the hallway, and I know he's looking at Kelsey's door.

I don't like that he's locked her in there. I was the only one to vote we not put her under house arrest.

"Be careful with your implications, Casey. What exactly are you trying to tell me?" Thad is peering at me with intensity.

I can't bring myself to say the words loud. So, I whisper. "What if it's Brax?"

# FORTY-TWO

## KELSEY

**3 Days to Christmas**

I pace around the room. My energy is frenetic—like a caged wild animal. My family, the unit of people who have always protected me and had my back growing up, has locked me in here. I am not in here by choice. But my palms are sweating, and my heart is racing. Still, I know what I have to do. I have to go back to that dreaded night when I lost everything.

I sink down to the floor where I left my notebook from my college classes. It's open to the page I was reading earlier, and my eyes fall on the words *dissociative fugue*. I start ruffling through them quickly. I don't have access to my therapist, Dr. Trina, but I have my PhD in psychology, and my next step is to find a job where I can take patients under supervision. What better way than to start with myself?

My finger finds the chapter section notes I'm looking for. "Repressed childhood memories due to trauma..." I read the entire section. Similar to dissociative amnesia, sometimes our minds can block traumatic experiences because we are unable to process them. This is no longer an option for me. I have no choice.

My theory is my actions today are directly affecting what is happening around us. That being around my family again after all those years of distance has caused me to regress to the time frame when I first moved in with my new adopted family, which was moments after my entire family was brutally murdered and ripped from my life.

"Here it is!" Triumphantly, I pause and read the section. "Journal writing with your nondominant hand while thinking about a traumatic experience in childhood can reveal truths that were evident to you back then. Warning, your memories will come from the perspective of a child at the age you were at the time."

I rescan my notes. Wasn't there some step-by-step process for prepping the patient on how to get into this mindset before starting this exercise? I blink as I stare into space. Meditation comes to mind. Clearing my head and getting into a centered place within myself sounds like a good first step.

But what about after I've uncovered the repressed memories. What will be my state of mind then? I'm just going to have to take care of myself now and put myself in a space where I feel safe and comfortable. I bite my lower lip so hard I'm surprised to feel the tang of blood. I clearly don't feel safe here.

"Okay..." I scramble to my feet and go through the clothes I brought with me. I put on my most worn and comfortable sweats and a pair of fuzzy socks. "Better."

I throw open the closet door to find a clutter of blankets, pillows, and old boxes. Were these my old things? Reverently, I paw through them until I find my old blankie. I pull it from underneath the heap, not caring how the rest of the pile topples over.

Next, I attack a box. I opened the lid and cough as dust flies into the air. I waved my hand around, hoping to settle the particles. I gasped softly as I see a small number of toys and stuffed animals from my childhood. I must have left them here during one of our trips and outgrown them enough that I didn't miss them for the entire next year.

I shove my hand inside and come out with Big Bear who had been my source of comfort for many years after joining my new family.

"Hi!" I squeeze him to my chest, in awe that the box seems to have protected him from the dust. His fur is still white. I take a deep breath in. He smells like—me, when I was little. I had this perfume that I'd begged Mom to get me once when we went to the mall. It was sweet and flowery.

I plunge my hand back into the box. "Yes!" My fingers close over the glass, octagon-shaped bottle. "Wow, I cannot believe I still have this!"

Leaving the chaos I uncovered, I kick the blanket and pillows back into the closet and close the doors, feeling like I might get busted, the same way I did when I was little, and I didn't really want to clean my room, just hide my mess.

I spray the perfume on me, grab Big Bear, and scramble up to my bed. I lean over the edge and stretch to reach my notebook and pen I left on the floor, remembering the days when we'd play games like that. *Don't let your feet touch the floor, there's molten lava below, but you have to grab your notebook before it catches on fire.*

I grab my notebook without leaving the bed. Points for me. Then I sit crisscross applesauce on top of my comforter on the bed I made when I woke up. Mom always made us make our bed before we could come down to breakfast. I close my eyes and think about that.

No, that doesn't sound right. Mom didn't care if Casey and I had messy beds. I wasn't thinking about my adoptive mom. I was thinking about my biological mom. Good. I conjure up a picture of my real mom. Like me, she had beautiful, long, flowing blond hair and vivid blue eyes. I wanted to look just like her. To be her. I felt like I was the luckiest girl alive.

We both felt like that. Kammy and I would giggle about how lucky we were long after the lights were out as we lay in bed at night. We would pull the comforter over our heads and tell each other all our secrets.

Daddy was pretty great, too. He was more serious than Mommy, and he worked a lot. But he was kind and played with us on the weekends. In those days, we were happy. So, why did they all leave me?

I wipe tears from the corner of my eyes. I shake my head. No, that's not right. They didn't leave me. They were murdered. They were taken from me. Still, I was so alone. Despite this new family who surrounded me afterward, I've felt alone ever since.

Tears flow, a steady stream at first, then harder and faster, soaking my sweatshirt as they roll down my neck. I let them come.

"It's okay to feel your feelings," I whisper to myself. "You are in a safe place."

I wrapped my arms around myself, giving myself a hug. This is good. I need to keep going. I open my eyes and put my pen on an empty notebook page with my left hand, which is nondominant. In slow, shaky writing, I begin to write.

*The bedroom was pitch-black. Kammy was snoring. Like always. But that's not what woke me up. I stared out into the hallway, trying to see. Then I heard something.*

*I heard a loud scream in the house. Then it cut off. Maybe Mom stubbed her toe going to the bathroom? I didn't believe that though. My stomach hurt. Like something was wrong.*

*Then I heard footsteps. They sounded like Dad's work boots, but why would Dad be walking around so late at night? What if it wasn't Dad?*

*My whole body shook as footsteps came closer to our room. I threw my comforter over my head and curled up into a ball. Maybe it would look like no one was here, and there was just a ball of covers.*

*The footsteps came closer. They stopped outside the room. I held my breath and tried to stay still. My body was shaking so hard, the covers might be moving.*

*Be like a statue, I thought. I squeezed my eyes shut tight and held my breath harder. The footsteps came into the room.*

*"Wakey, wakey little girlie!" It was a man's voice.*

*A surprised cry sounded from my sister. Her bed was next to mine. We begged Mom and Dad to put them together, but they wanted us to be in our own beds.*

*Hot pee spilled out of me as I wet the bed. I started crying softly.*

*Kammy! I didn't warn her. I'd just hid on my bed!*

*Kammy screamed so loud, it hurt my ears. Then she stopped, and I could hear gurgling and gasping.*

*Then, I heard nothing. I lay there not moving for so long I thought he was gone. I had to save her. I could fix it. I would keep Kammy alive. We were twins. If she died, I would die. I was still alive.*

*I threw the covers off me. Cool air rushed in. It had been hot under there. I had held my breath a long, long time. I gasped for air.*

*But the man was still there. It was so black in the room, I couldn't see him. He turned, and I saw the white in his eyes. He looked surprised. Then, he was on me, holding me down. It was so fast, I couldn't fight. He was holding me down. The metal was cold, and the knife was sharp. He pressed it against my neck. I started gagging.*

*"So, you're the smart one, huh, girlie? You thought you could hide while I killed your sister? That's not very nice. You should have stayed hidden. You—"*

*"Police, freeze!"*

*The knife clattered to the floor, and the man stood up with his hands in the air.*

*"Kammy!" I went to her bed to look at her. Her eyes were closed. I shook her. She didn't wake up. I could see a dark stain everywhere.*

*Then the light turned on. I could hear the police. I knew they had the bad man. I didn't care. I only cared about Kammy. Red stained her blankets. It poured out of her neck.*

*"Help!" I screamed. I put my hands in the blood and tried to scoop it up and put it back in. I didn't work. Then I tried to cover it up. I put my hands on her neck. Then I wanted to hide it. I couldn't stand to see it. So, I grabbed a blanket and put it on Kammy's neck.*

*I held it there until someone patted my shoulder.*

*"Honey, we need to look at your sister."*

*"She's dead," I cried because I couldn't feel it anymore.*

*Our twin bond was gone. I could tell. She was my twin sister and our bond was gone.*

*"Honey, I need to get in here, okay?" Gentle hands moved me from Kammy's side. I felt cold.*

*"No!" I screamed. "No!"*

*"Take her to the ambulance to check her over," the nice lady said.*

*Someone lifted me in the air. "No!" I started kicking my feet and flailing my body.*

*"We need to look at you." A man held me in his arms. Not the man who killed my sister.*

*I was crying so hard, I don't think I answered. I was being carried away.*

*"Hey!" the nice lady said. "She's alive!"*

*The next thing I remembered was waking up in a hospital.*

*A nurse came in. "You're awake!"*

*"I want my mom and dad," I told her. My throat hurt. I put a hand up and felt a bandage. Then I cried harder because I remembered my sister was dead.*

*The nurse looked sympathetic and came to sit on my bed. "They're gone, sweetie. Your family is gone."*

*"All of them?" The tears would never stop falling.*

*She nodded. "I'm so sorry."*

*I turned my head and looked at the white wall of the hospital.*

*I was all alone now.*

My hand cramped so I threw down my pen. It was so hard to read my writing, but I desperately scanned back over the page.

"No, no, no," I muttered. "That's not right. Kammy was dead. He killed her in her bed."

And yet, I had written that a nice lady had yelled, *She's alive!* with my nondominant hand.

"Kammy's not alive."

A sudden movement came from my connected bathroom. A woman who looked like me, but stronger and fitter filled the doorframe as if she's been hiding behind the bathroom door this whole time.

"And yet, here I am. Hello, sister."

# FORTY-THREE

## KELSEY

**3 Days to Christmas**

Excitement and joy and feelings of completeness flood into my body, and my first instinct is to jump up and give Kammy a hug and never let go. I move off my bed to do exactly that, but I stop abruptly. Something is wrong. A new feeling downloads into my gut. As I stare into the eyes that mirror my own, I know that something is *off*. Her eyes are the same color as mine, but they are rimmed in a black that give off a dark and sinister vibe.

My twin senses are on fire in a way I used to think I missed after Kammy was murdered. I've never been one to characterize people as good, bad, or evil. But as I look at Kammy, something in me recoils, and I know she is not the same as when we were five years old. In fact, it occurs to me that she's lived the majority of her life without me, and I don't even know what that consisted of.

"How are you... here?" The words come out stuttered because my brain is having a hard time forming coherent thoughts.

She smiles, but it's not one of joy or reconciliation. It's sardonic and tilts in a smirk that screams *danger*.

"It turns out, you saved me, sister." Her voice is raspy and deeper than mine. I blink a few times, not expecting that sound to come out of her. She flutters her fingertips over her neck, and that's when I see it. An angry red scar that has no doubt faded with age. But it's there as clear as she is standing in front of me.

"Then *why*... where did you...?"

Kammy's words are clipped and sharp. "Where did I go *after* I survived?" Her eyes harden and go flat. Her face turns fuchsia. "They ripped us apart. I didn't have the luxury of a beautiful childhood with parents who loved me. I was placed in the system. People like your sister, Ellen, put me with families they thought would be good for me. Families who abused me in every possible way and then dumped me back into the system."

My mind worked to understand her words and read what she was not saying while assessing her emotional state.

"Oh my God!" The words fall out of my mouth before I can stop them as the realization slams into me, and my whole body flushes ice cold into my veins. "You killed her, didn't you? You killed Ellen?"

She tsked her tongue. "That's the wrong question, sister." Then Kammy is on me. Fast as a cheetah and far stronger than me, she wrestles me to the ground. My head hits the corner of the bed post frame on my way down. For a minute, I see black with stars circling me.

She has weight on me. Not a lot, but it appears to be all muscle as I buck against her, thrashing my body and trying hard to throw her off. I shut down my emotions and just react. A sudden calm enters my brain, and my body feels surreal, like I am watching from outside myself. Survival mode. I know it well.

Kammy laughs as she positions her left arm against my throat. The sound is unhinged and terrible. Like she has already won and is waiting for me to catch up. It is half a minute before I know why. From nowhere, maybe her back pocket, she has produced a knife. In her right hand, she now holds it above my jugular with so much pressure on my throat, I can't breathe. This is different from my panic attacks. This is calculated. Kammy is cutting off my oxygen. My own twin sister is trying to kill me.

"Wait!" I grunt, each word an effort as I struggle to push her arm away. "After all this time. We're finally reunited. This is what you want to do?" The desperation in my voice betrays my state of mind.

"Don't try to manipulate me! This is the plan. It was always the plan. Your family..." Kammy presses harder, her arm cutting off my oxygen. The sharp edge of the knife is cold against my throat.

I try to jerk back, but there's nowhere for my head to go.

*Oh God!* "My family..." *She's going to kill me and go kill them!*

"Your family needs to believe the right sister died. My whole life has been horrible. But this is your chance to help make it right. So, stop struggling!"

I'm using both hands now to push away the knife, but it's not working. She's so much stronger than me. She puts more pressure on her arm, cutting off my ability breathe or speak. I can feel a sharp sting as the tip of the blade nicks the top layer of my skin.

In this moment, it occurs to me that she is going to kill me whether I fight back or freeze in fear. What is more important is my family downstairs. Protecting them at all costs. I have to be alive to do that.

I grab her sides, expecting to find excess skin and padding that often bunches on women. I know I have it. I grab hard. Only she doesn't have any fat there. But I pinch and squeeze so hard that I feel my nails puncture her skin through the fabric of her shirt.

She cries out in surprise and reacts, falling sideways.

Siezing the advantage, I roll us so I'm now on top of Kammy. It is sheer adrenaline and willpower that enables me as I grab and hold her right hand. She is still gripping the knife so hard her knuckles are white. I pick her hand up and slam it back down, once, twice, three times until her strong grip finally goes slack, and the knife skids across the room.

I hear a slam against my bedroom door, but I know it is locked.

I scream loudly. "Help!" Then I hear the sweetest words I've ever heard.

"Police! Coming in!"

"Help me!" I call again.

"Stand back!" The door crashes open.

I don't have to look behind me to know there will be a uniformed officer. Kammy and I are frozen on the ground when I realize the positioning of our bodies. I am pinning Kammy down with my hands firmly holding hers over her head. The knife has skid on the floor just out of our reach.

Kammy realizes it as well. She lets out a sudden wail.

"Thank God you're here, officer! Kelsey was trying to kill me!"

My mouth falls open, and I gasp, unable to form words. I am all too aware of what this looks like. I raise my hands in complete submission. I can explain, right?

Kammy jumps up, runs, and hugs the officer. "Thank you. Ohmigod, I thought she was going to kill me!"

The officer detangles the now crying Kammy from around his waist and levels me with hard eyes. "Miss?"

"Wait! Please..." A tear forms and leaks down my cheek, followed by more. "I thought she was dead. This whole time, I thought—"

The officer's authoritative voice matches his commanding stature. "You're going to have to come with me."

Panic spirals inside. *What if he left Kammy with my unsuspecting family?* My family would be able to recognize the difference between me and Kammy, right?

"Her fingerprints will be on the knife." I point to the knife laying feet away. "If she's innocent, why would her fingerprints be on the knife?"

The officer, whose hand is still holding onto Kammy's muscular arm, hesitates, seeming to think through my words.

In sheer desperation, words vomit out of me. "Are you here because of the nine-one-one call?"

The officer nods slowly. "We would have been here sooner, but we couldn't pinpoint your location. Just the cell number."

"That was me. I called you."

"Oh, come on. It was from me, and you know it," Kammy protests.

"What's the phone number it came from?" I challenged.

"It was—I used your phone—"

I turn to the officer. "Can you verify the number that called?"

The officer nods slowly, his eyes bouncing from me to Kammy and back.

"Okay." I turned to the bed but remember Thad has Ellen's phone now.

"Woah! Don't move. Put your hands in the air!" The officer booms.

I obey. "I was just going to grab the phone that made the phone call. It was between my mattresses."

"Would that be Ellen's phone?" Kammy smirked. She turns to the officer. "That phone belongs to the dead girl lying down below."

"How do you know where Ellen is?"

"I—you can see her! How sick are you all to just leave your sister's body by the woodshed?" Kammy sputters, deflecting.

"Okay, both of you. You're coming with me." His hand clamps onto my arm, and he leads me with one hand and Kammy with the other, downstairs. At the top of the stairs, the officer stops and calls down to another officer who is taking statements from my family.

Every family member looks up at us, and I watch the shock register on each of their faces. I don't know how Kammy got by us all, but it's clear they are as shocked as I am by the revelation that she is still alive.

The officer walks us down the stairs. Mom walks forward and studies Kammy with clear distaste of her face. Then she sticks her finger in her face.

"You. It was you. Not Kelsey. You were alive all along and causing all this trouble." Mom's eyes narrow as she sizes Kammy up. "You were up in the attic this whole time, weren't you? I knew I heard you after everyone was sleeping!"

The realization of her words hit me like a sledgehammer. Was Kammy running around appearing to my family and creating contention, waiting on her chance to destroy us all?

Sudden tears spring to my eyes as relief floods through me. Mom is standing up for me. She knows who I am and is protecting me. It was so stressful having Mom be so angry at me this week. I glance around at Thad, Melly, Casey, and Dad. All of them look apologetic. I'm innocent, and they all know it now.

"I'm sorry, Kelsey. This makes more sense. You would never have done those awful things—"

"Oh, shut up, old woman!" Kammy snaps. In an unexpected, but fast movement, Kammy stomps on the officer's insole and elbows him in the stomach. She grabs Casey, who is standing the closest to her and places her arms around Casey's neck in a sleeper hold.

"Nobody move or I'll break her neck!" Kammy screams. Her voice is shrill, but raspy at the same time. Her eyes are wild, and the black that rims her pupils are wide. Her face is in a full smirk, giving her the appearance of a deranged convict. How could I have ever thought my family would mix us up?

"Nope," Casey says, and before anyone can react, she pushes Kammy's arm away, backs herself up into my psychotic twin, and flips her over her shoulder.

Kammy sprawls on her back on the living room floor like a starfish, and I can tell it knocked the wind out of her.

"Learned that in women's self-defense!" Casey crows triumphantly and bounces on her toes like a fighter.

"Let's go." An officer picks Kammy off the floor and

cuffs her. "You are both taking a ride to the station while we sort this out."

"Both?" Thad interjects, pointing to Kammy. "I mean, clearly you have the correct suspect."

"Yes, we'll get this sorted out at the station," the officer states in a voice of final authority. The officers drop their voices, but I can still hear their discussion.

"We need to get another vehicle up here to transport the second suspect."

"We barely made it up here ourselves with the weather—"

"You're right. We'll have to make an exception."

*Sorry*, Casey mouths to me.

Dad shakes his head with sadness filling his eyes.

Mom runs up to me and throws her arms around my neck. "You come right back here when this misunderstanding is cleared up, Kelsey Kristine!"

Helplessly, I allow the man to hand me off to the other officer who handcuffs my hands in front of me and leads me and Kammy out of the house.

I had fantasized my whole life about a reunion with my twin sister. But this was never the way the fantasy went down.

# FORTY-FOUR

## KELSEY

**3 Days to Christmas**

It's surreal to be in handcuffs next to my twin sister. We are in the back seat of a police cruiser. My hands are cuffed to the left door. Kammy's hands are cuffed to the right door, leaving a seat between us. The snow crunches beneath the tires, and the vehicle slips a bit as it makes its way slowly down the mountain. I notice how slow the officer is driving. Snowplows don't come up the mountain in this weather. They never have.

I keep sneaking peeks at Kammy because I still can't believe she's alive. I want to ask her how we got separated and why no one ever put the two of us back together. I have so many questions. Why did they allow me to think Kammy was dead? I can't understand why she waited until now to reveal herself.

Instead I ask, "Were you really living in the attic space this whole time?"

Kammy smirks at me and nods. "This week, yeah. But I've been following your family around for years."

"No talking!" An officer snaps.

Kammy rolls her eyes before returning to looking out the window.

It seems like Kammy never grew up after I watched her die when I was five years old. But she's not the same at all. My emotions are a jumbled mess. I should feel elated that Kammy didn't die. Instead, I feel sorrow for who she's become. She is the opposite of me in every possible way. That special bond scientists describe that happens between twins isn't there. We aren't connected anymore. I don't want to draw near her. I'm repulsed by her.

At that thought, shame floods me like an adrenaline dump. She's the exact sort of client, that as a psychologist, I will want to help some day. A person who is a product of the system, living and operating under false beliefs. That would have been me had I not been adopted into a kind, loving family. How odd to have that realization now, when I spent the majority of my college years feeling like a survivor of childhood chaos. I look at Kammy, and I know now that my life could have been so much worse.

As I sneak one more glance at Kammy, I note our physical differences. She seems comfortable in her lean but muscular frame. Or maybe she's just comfortable in the back of a police car. I am thin but have no muscle definition. She's wearing athletic clothes. I am wearing jeans, a sweatshirt, and fuzzy socks. Her hair has an accidental ombre thing happening, which looks like she tried to dye her hair brown, but it grew out, and the blond has come in strong. It's edgy, but it's working for her. My blond hair hasn't been dyed because I could never afford it in college. Besides, I like my natural color. I realize where the officers might have their work cut out for them in proving which one of us killed my sister, Ellen, and who attacked Thad, but I know my family can help clear that up. I tell myself there's no chance the officers will mix us up.

I'm more worried that when they investigate the crimes, they will find evidence that I was the perpetrator. Even though the actual criminal sits right next to me. Still, officers get it wrong all the time, don't they? The wrong people get sent to jail based on the strength of a case a lawyer can build.

I'm staring out the window at the wintery wonderland illuminated by the officer's headlights. The miserable snow stretches as far as we can see before the tree line cuts off our view, just past the illuminated roads. That's when I see it.

"Stop the car!" I shout.

"What the—" The officer in the passenger seat grumbles, but he sees the vehicle at the same time. Did they miss that on the trip coming up the mountain? The cruiser grounds to a slippery halt.

Mom and Dad's station wagon is sitting perpendicular to the road. The angle is all wrong, and it looks like the car slid for about fifty feet down the mountain before it came to a stop.

"Can you please check to see if my brother-in-law is in that car?" I request. "He left around two yesterday to get help. That's the car he was driving."

I watch as the officer in the passenger seat turns on a flashlight and carefully walks sideways down the slick hill.

He flashes his light all around, and I can see from here that the car is vacant. *That's odd.* Where is Brax?

The officer gets back in the car. As he turns to me, I see Officer Lexton embroidered on a patch.

He looks back at me. "Car's empty."

"Do you have cell service here?" I wonder.

He pulls out his phone and looks. He glances back at me and nods. "Now, stop asking me questions."

This reminds me that I'm a prisoner. Still, Officer Lexton seems kind, and his brown eyes make him look approachable.

The driver continues down the hill.

"Do you have a way to know if EMTs were dispatched? I need to find the driver." I know I'm pushing my luck.

Officer Lexton turns around again. "Look, you're a prisoner. I'm not supposed to converse with you. I can check with emergency dispatch when we get to the station. If you're cleared, we'll talk about this further."

*If I'm cleared.* Though he is being nice to me, he doesn't know if I'm innocent or guilty. This sends a chill up my spine.

What will happen to me if they find me guilty?

# FORTY-FIVE

## KELSEY

**3 Days to Christmas**

"Well, this is the cherry on top of a terrible fucking life," Kammy snaps at me as they fingerprint her. "Hope this ruins yours."

I watch wordlessly as they lead her away and wonder if I will ever see her again, but the feeling in my gut says that I will not.

After fingerprinting me and taking my mugshot, the officer places me in an interrogation room and reads me my rights. He tells me I'm here because I'm suspected of murder, assault and battery, and arson. He asks if I under-stand, and I nod as I gulp loudly. He tells me he'll be right back and leaves, closing a door behind him that I know is locking me in.

Until now, I've only seen one of these types of rooms on TV. It's eerily similar to those cop shows Casey loved and made me watch with her growing up. The lighting is a bit too bright. There are no windows in the room. I can only see my reflection in the glass, but I know it's likely there are officers on the other side observing my behavior. I know what they will see. Though I haven't launched into a full-out panic attack, I am nervous, and I am sure my body language reflects that. The shake in my hands is obvious. My siblings always told me growing up that I blink a lot and stare too much. That still happens on occasion as an adult. I'm afraid they will determine that I am the one who is trying to harm my family based on my strange behavior.

Eventually, Officer Lexton enters the room. It seems like hours have passed, but it's probably been fifteen or twenty minutes.

He throws a yellow legal pad on the table and sits across from me. "Ms. Caper, I need to ask you some questions."

There's no reason to be uncooperative. "Sure."

"I understand you were the one who discovered your sister Ellen's body?" Lexton begins, looking at me expectantly.

I nod. Tears spring to my eyes.

"Tell me about that." His eyes soften. "Take your time."

"Uh." I sniffle and try to get my emotions under control. Talking about it makes it more real, not a bizarre nightmare. "I was mad at my mom and needed a moment to cool down, so I went outside."

"Literally, cool down, huh?" He murmurs, making a note on the pad. "When was this?"

I think back, stunned by how much has happened in such a short period of time. "Three days, I think."

"And did you cool down?"

"Yes."

"Continue."

I feel my cheeks flush as embarrassment takes over. "I laid back in the snow. Made a snow angel—"

"A snow angel?" Lexton's mouth quirks. His eyes roam over me. "You don't strike me as a snow angel type."

I can only surmise what my rigid posture portrays, and I want to object, but he's right.

"I'm not." I sigh. "Okay, I just got my degree in psychology, and I can only explain it like this. Coming home to my family triggered my inner child. More than once. I got mad, stormed out, cooled down, and made a snow angel." I didn't realize how that would sound until I said it aloud.

To his credit, Officer Lexton does not laugh or poke fun. He stares at me for half a second and nods his head. "Okay, you made a snow angel. Then what?"

"As I was rolling my head, something caught my attention. It was the contrast of red against the snow. Then, I saw my sister." Tears spill, and I attempt to wipe them away.

"Then?"

"I started screaming."

"Okay, let's back up. What time did your flight arrive?"

"Three ten p.m. I got home around four in the afternoon."

"Okay, we'll check the timeline with the airport."

"Of course." He needs to establish a timeline. I took a criminology class in college.

"Let's talk about how she was killed." Lexton looks at me, waiting for my reaction.

My mind sees the knife laying next to my sister, the wound at her neck, and the frozen puddle of blood on the ground behind her. The image is vivid. I feel my stomach turn. I tell him what I found when I got closer.

"Did it remind you of anything?" His question is a leading one, but I willingly play into it. I have nothing to hide.

"It's how my sister was killed when we were five."

"But she wasn't killed," Lexton corrects.

"A fact I just learned less than two hours ago." I shake my head, still reeling from that epiphany.

"That must have been surreal."

"Yes."

"Weren't you happy to see her?" Lexton asks.

"At first. Until my brain made some connections, and I suspected she was behind all of this."

"All of this?" Lexton rolls his wrist, making a motion to continue.

"Ellen's murder, Thad's attack, and the house fire," I list. Then I hesitate. "She told me my family needed to think the right sister died. I think she was trying to frame me. I found the key to the snowmobile in my coat pocket and Ellen's phone under my bed mattress."

Officer Lexton makes note. "What's the significance of the snowmobile key?"

"Someone had cut the gas line so there was no way to use it. This was after the key went missing. My brother and I had used the snowmobile when we first got home but couldn't find it after we found Ellen."

"Why did you use the snowmobile?" he asked.

"To get a cell signal. Our phones don't work up there in this weather. We knew Ellen wasn't there and needed to make sure she was okay. After she was found, we wanted to call for help, but the snowmobile had been sabotaged."

"Ah." Lexton clicks his tongue.

I finally feel relieved, like Lexton might be coming around to trusting me when there's a knock at the door.

"Perfect timing," Lexton says.

Two plain clothes officials step into the room. They are dressed casually, though a pretty woman with auburn hair pulled back into a messy ponytail is wearing a jacket that says *US Marshal*. My eyes widen as I read it three more times, and I know I'm in more trouble than I thought.

They've called in the US Marshals.

# FORTY-SIX

## KELSEY

**3 Days to Christmas**

"Kelsey Caper, this is US Marshal Mak Cunningham." Officer Lexton pauses as the woman takes a seat across from me and reaches out a hand. "And this is US Marshal Stephen Wilton."

"Nice to meet you." Marshal Wilton remains standing but offers his hand as well. He's very good-looking with wavy blond hair and striking blue eyes. I can tell from the way he fills out his clothes that he's muscular and fit.

My eyes find Officer Lexton and hesitate. He's staring at me with a quizzical look on his face like I'm a puzzle he needs to solve. He's handsome too, though a complete opposite to Marshal Wilton. Lexton has dark hair and brown eyes. He's fit too, though he looks more like a body builder than a cop. Now that he's not interrogating me, it's like I'm seeing him differently. He looks young, maybe my age.

Marshal Mak clears her throat, and I pull my attention from Lexton. She smiles and has kind eyes, but I realize it's likely a ploy to disarm me. It's okay, I'll tell the truth. I have nothing to hide.

"Ms. Caper—"

"Please, call me Kelsey."

"Okay, Kelsey. Do you know why we're here?" Mak asks.

I knit my eyebrows together, and my confusion must show on my face. "Is this a trick question?"

Mak shares a smile with Wilton, and I feel like I'm missing something.

"Let me rephrase and explain." She sweeps a hand to Lexton. "It's Officer Lexton's job to ask you questions and take your statement about what's been happening up on the mountain with your family for the past few days. But US Marshals are called in when there's a repeat criminal who has evaded the law for too long. Our purpose is to apprehend said criminal and bring him—"

"Or her," Wilton interrupted.

Mak smirks at him. "I was getting to that. *Or her* to justice."

"Okay. I'm not sure what this has to do with me," I say carefully. My pulse speeds up at the thought. Do they think I am a big criminal?

"Tell me about your relationship with your sister, Kammy Simmons," Mak probes gently. Her eyes are soft, almost with compassion in them. It doesn't seem to be an act. I decide I like her.

My heart burns at the mention of our family name,

Simmons. Kammy kept it all these years. "I thought my sister was dead until about two hours ago. The last memory I have before that is from when I was five years old, and a man slit her throat in front of me. It was a shock when she showed up in my room earlier today."

"So, you haven't had any contact at all with your sister through the years?" Mak questions.

"No," I confirm.

Mak regards me in silence. Wilton sits in the other chair and starts thumbing through a file like he's looking for something to corroborate my story. He pulls out a yellowed official looking document and puts it on the table between him and Mak.

Mak's eyes scan the page. She inhales and shakes her head sadly.

"What's going on?" I demand.

"You might as well know that Kammy Simmons is wanted in multiple states for offenses ranging from theft to arson, and escalating to murder," Mak announces.

I gasp, truly shocked. This woman who shares my DNA is a criminal. My pulse picks up as I realize her DNA might flag mine. I make a mental note to ask about that. How will they be able to differentiate between us?

Marshal Wilton gives her a chastising look, and I determine I am not supposed to know those things. I'm glad Mak broke protocol.

"Wilton and I have been called in to apprehend her. We're taking her to the state where it all began to stand trial. So, you can understand why we need to ask these questions." Mak taps her short fingernails on the table.

I speak aloud. "You have to make sure I wasn't an accomplice."

"Were you?" Wilton's blue eyes are piercing, and though I'm innocent, I squirm a little under his gaze.

"No."

"Has anyone ever anonymously reached out to you for any reason over the years?" Wilton asks.

I start to shake my head but stop. "Not me. But multiple family members accused me of erratic behavior, swearing I said and did things I have no memory of. I haven't seen any of them since I graduated with my master's. Now, I think she might have been showing up and harassing them."

"Okay," Mak says.

Wilton makes a note for his file. They are building a case against Kammy.

I look at Officer Lexton. "Does this mean I am free to go?"

"Not quite." Lexton steps forward. "There's a matter of fingerprints, DNA, and following the evidence. We'll need you to stay here a night or two until we can clear you."

My heart sinks. I have to sleep in jail?

Lexton gives me an apologetic shrug. He's just doing his job. I understand.

There's still something I don't understand. "Can I ask a question?"

Mak nods. "Of course."

"Why didn't anyone try to reunite me and Kammy when we were younger?"

Mak sighs and looks at Wilton, gesturing toward the file. "You want to take this one?"

Wilton sits up. "All law enforcement officers do things differently. I don't agree with how they handled this one. Your sister saw her attacker. You didn't. At least, you had no memory of it if you did. They kept Kammy in protection and reported her dead so they could have access to her at any point. Granted, the memory of a five-year-old is flawed, but in this case, it was what they used to put him away."

"The murderer was brought to justice?" Something in my heart lightens. I always feared that he would come back for me and finish the job he started.

Mak's eyes widen. "Do you really not know?"

I shake my head.

Wilton clears his throat. "With you being a minor, the information would go to your adopted parents. Your uncle, Brad Simmons, was convinced your grandmother was going to leave everything to your father, so he killed your parents, hurt your sister, and started on you." He points to the faint scar I have on my neck. It's not nearly as pronounced as my sister's. I reach up to touch it, and my fingers come away with flakes of dried blood. I forgot Kammy nicked me with the knife. "He was convicted to life without parole."

I feel the color leave my face, and I suddenly feel like a noodle with all my energy going toward holding up my body. That's why they could use a young girl's testimony. Kammy could identify her own uncle at that age. Not to mention, the police caught him in the act with me.

"I didn't know," I whisper.

"I'm sorry we had to be the ones to tell you." Mak gives me a sympathetic look.

I grit my teeth. When I get out of here, there's going to be a long discussion with my mom about the damage of withholding information. It's time to clear the air. For good. If I've learned anything this vacation, it's that the past doesn't have to define us, but it can give us a key to understanding why we are who we are today.

# FORTY-SEVEN

## KELSEY

**3 Days to Christmas**

As I'm led back to a cell where I will stay until I'm cleared, I have the sad realization. Kammy was only a child when the authorities used her to get information about the murderer of our family. I feel conflicted—sorry for Kammy, but furious over the choices she made. I'm brought to the present as the cell slams shut behind me with dreadful finality. I am imprisoned for choices I did not make.

Lexton hesitates outside my cell. "I'm sorry I have to do this."

I study his eyes, thinking about how kind they are. He shoves his hands in his pockets and looks like he doesn't want to leave. Maybe he doesn't want to leave me.

"You don't think I'm guilty, do you?" I breathe. I put my hands on the bars and draw myself closer.

Lexton steps closer, too. We are suddenly only separated by this jail cell. "I don't."

"How will you—" I stop and think about how to best ask this question. "Kammy and I are identical. Will her DNA show up differently than mine?"

Lexton slowly shakes his head. "Well, there are advanced genetic tests that can show small mutations, but we would have to send them off, and it could take months to get the results."

My eyes widen at the implications. "Then how will you—"

"Fingerprints." He rubs the stubble on his chin. Then he crosses his fingers.

"If she left any," I huff out.

"Remember that she has previous offenses. She's going away no matter what. We establish a time of death, and if you have an alibi for the time frame, you are clear. Your brother initially stated that you attacked him, but I bet he'll retract that. With the absence of evidence, you'll be cleared," he encourages. The dimple on the right side of his face indents with his small comforting smile.

I search Lexton's face. He's very attractive. "So, there's no way a court will find me guilty?"

"Are you guilty?" he asks.

"No, I'm just worried..." I pause and look away, wondering why I suddenly feel like spilling my secrets to this man.

His brows knit like he's worried I'm going to confess something. Most law officials would be excited by this prospect, but he already looks disappointed.

"It's just that I realize now I never appreciated my

family. They were loud and chaotic, but they were mine. Kammy had nothing and nobody."

"None of that is your fault, and Kammy could have chosen differently—better," Lexton says.

I feel so ungrateful. "Still, I could have had it so much worse."

"You aren't wrong," Lexton agrees. "Kammy was in witness protection since she was young, and the authorities basically treated her like a tool. She started running away and living on the streets as a teenager before anyone thought to provide her with help or resources."

I am hanging on his words. "How do you know all this?"

"It's in the file. The US Marshals are thorough. They seem to know everything about Kammy." Lexton points over his shoulder toward the office.

"Will they take her childhood into consideration when determining her sentence?" I feel concerned about this woman who once was as close to me as my own arm.

Lexton shrugs. "Perhaps. They think she began by committing petty theft to survive."

I am not surprised, just sad. I am convinced she killed Ellen, attacked Thad, and attempted to burn the cabin down with my family inside it. I don't need my psychology degree to know plenty of people with bad childhoods become survivors and choose to be strong in the face of adversity. Kammy chose resentment and revenge.

I doubt I'll see her again. Especially since she's being transported out of state. But one question plagues me.

"Is there any chance she will go free and come after my family again?"

"It's doubtful." Lexton shifts on his feet. "I need to go get my reports done. But I'll bring you dinner before I head out. Any special requests?"

I smile at his kindness. "I'm not picky. I do try to eat healthy, but I'll take what I can get here."

Lexton smiles brightly, and because I've had one of the most stressful days of my life, I feel grateful for him.

"A head of lettuce it is." With that he walks away.

I smile after him, despite the fact that I have to spend the night in a jail cell—maybe longer.

# FORTY-EIGHT

CASEY

**3 Days to Christmas**

It's the darndest thing. Shortly after they took Kelsey and Kammy away, a fact that we're all still reeling from, our Wi-Fi started working again. The police explained that they found a Wi-Fi jammer, which is an illegal device. Whoever killed Ellen—which is no mystery, we all believe it was Kammy—used the jammer to make sure we couldn't get help.

The police and crime scene techs have been here investigating Ellen's murder. They've dusted for prints, presumably looking for Kammy's, because we all have prints all over this house.

The paramedics arrived and checked Thad. He's not in

an acute condition, thanks to Melly. We all rode down to the hospital so Thad could get a more thorough examination. It turns out he has a depressed fracture, and he needs surgery to repair part of the bone closer to his brain. The doctors were hesitant since it's been over twenty-four hours but said Melly's care kept it from getting infected. Once they determined his physical state was stable, they rushed him into surgery prep. Melly is with him as we speak.

Speaking of the hospital, that's where they found Brax. First, they found Mom and Dad's car wrecked in a precarious position on the mountain. After the accident, Brax came to enough to call for an ambulance which arrived and took him down the mountain. Brax's injuries could have been way worse. He broke his arm, and he hit his head hard enough that he had some swelling in his brain. He had to have osmotherapy surgery to drain fluid. I'm sad I wasn't there for his recovery. When he woke, he tried to reach out, but he couldn't get through to us on account of the Wi-Fi issue.

After I hitched a ride down the mountain with the ambulance, they took me right to Brax. We're staying in the hospital for observation, but the doctor says they will release him soon. They're shooting for Christmas Eve.

I look at Brax, who is resting peacefully in his hospital bed. He's snoring softly, and I rub my still-flat stomach as I gaze at him. He's far from perfect, but he's going to be an amazing father. He risked his life in that god-awful weather to get us help, and I bet he would do it again tomorrow.

I feel so guilty for the assumptions I made about him. Brax didn't kill Ellen. Thad pointed out that the knife I found in Brax's luggage wasn't the murder weapon. When I casually asked Brax about the blood on the knife, he said he cut himself cleaning his fingernails. That's so Brax, I could almost see it. He said he used the match to step outside and smoke a joint the first night we were there. His lighter had stopped working. I giggled when he told me. He couldn't wait longer than a day before lighting up.

When I asked him the questions, Brax looked at me weird but didn't press. That's something I love about Brax. He's simple and takes things for face value. I hate that I let doubt enter my mind.

I never want to be in that position again and I fidget as I think about Kelsey locked up in that jail cell.

I had hoped this vacation would give us all a chance to start over—new beginnings. I have glimpses of hope for that in the future. But for now, Christmas Eve is tomorrow, and I just want our family to be healthy and back together again.

That's my new Christmas wish.

# FORTY-NINE

## THAD

**3 Days to Christmas**

I'd be lying if I said I wasn't nervous about this *procedure*, as they keep calling it. I have what they call a depressed fracture. Though a doctor has assured me that mine will be more *reconstructive*, the fact is, I'm having brain surgery. That would make anyone nervous.

When the doctor hears about how I fought the fire a day after I woke, he laughs. He tells me I must have a high tolerance to pain because most brain trauma victims suffer from dizziness and headaches. When he says that, I glance sheepishly at Melly.

"I knew it!" she declares. "I kept asking you if you felt alright, and you said you were fine. You were *not* fine!"

I shrug. "I was hopped up on adrenaline. Fire is what I do. I couldn't let anything happen to you guys."

Once I'm prepped for surgery and waiting for the anesthesia to kick in, I glance at my wife.

"Melly." I gently catch her wrist and pull her closer. She bends over me. Her hair so close to my face, it tickles me. "Thank you."

"Of course." Her eyes soften, but she regards me stiffly. I've decided to trust her again after her unfaithfulness, and I need to do this while I'm still coherent. She's more than proved herself. My whole family told me she never left my side while I was unconscious.

"I want to try again. To start over." I rub the inside of her wrist.

"You did say you would go to counseling with me," she answers carefully.

I wonder if she's afraid to hope.

"I want the whole thing with no reservations. I want us back. And yes, I'll go to counseling. I want to work on prioritizing you and us."

Tears fill her eyes, and she hugs me the best she can around my IV and tubes. "You're not just saying that because you think you might die, are you?"

I laugh. "No."

"And you aren't high right now, are you?" She waves a hand over my face.

"No. But I do think life is too short, Melly."

She sighs. "I couldn't agree more." She puts her hand in mine and waits as the medicine kicks in. I don't remember being wheeled into surgery, and I don't remember the procedure itself. All I know is Melly is there when I wake up. It's the most beautiful sight I've ever seen.

I'm going to be okay. We're going to be okay. We will survive this dark Christmas.

# FIFTY

**Christmas Day**

I gaze around the Christmas tree at my family, feeling grateful to be back home. It's a Christmas miracle. We all made it home, despite surgeries, injuries, and jail time. Thad was released yesterday after a less invasive procedure than they originally thought he'd have. He's healing well, and his head isn't dented in anymore. He's lounging on the couch, curled up next to Melly. My heart warms at the sight.

Brax, while sporting a cast on one arm, is relatively unharmed. He has instructions to watch for headache and dizziness, but his hit to the head was already healing before we found him. He's sitting on the floor in front of Casey, who is sitting crisscross applesauce, still in her jammies because, according to her, if you can't wear jammies on Christmas morning, when can you?

I'm sitting next to Casey. We finally got that time to reconnect. We stayed up most of the night, talking in front of the warm fireplace, drinking hot cocoa. We laughed over silly baby names, and I can't wait to know what they decide when the baby is born. We made promises not to let our relationship drift any further.

I gaze fondly at Mom and Dad. I had a long talk with them when I got back about the importance of not with-holding information. I explained that while I understood that Mom was trying to protect me, the information that my uncle had killed my parents and attempted to kill us girls could have been vital. While it's true that he has life in prison, what if he had broken out and shown up when I was in college? Prison breaks happen, right? More impor-tantly, I could have rested easier knowing the murderer was in prison. Mom still doesn't like it, but she promised to try to be more open about the past.

Our presents have been opened, and we are relaxing, cups of coffee in hand as the last of the brunch food cooking in the oven releases tantalizing aromas that waft in the air. There's a quiche and blueberry muffins. My stomach grum-bles in response.

I half expect one of my siblings to tease me about it, but before I can say anything, there is a knock at the front door. I immediately get up to answer, but I feel a knot of worry in my stomach. I glance around and see the concern on every-one's faces.

There's no peephole, so I'm surprised to find Officer Lexton at my door. Sam, as he told me to call him. When he brought me food that first night, he pulled up a chair, and we talked for hours after his shift ended. It was unexpected, but nice.

Now, Sam stands with his arms full of presents and a smile on his face.

Immediately, I grab a few from the top of his pile. "What's this?"

He follows me back inside. "These were found in the woodshed, and we had to take them to process them for evidence. I think they were your sister's Christmas gifts to all of you."

I gasp and tears spring to my eyes. My family, who can hear our conversation, is listening with rapt interest. I glance around at them. It's like Christmas presents from the beyond. Ellen's last *I love to you* to her family.

"Would you like to stay?" I ask Sam.

He puts the presents down. "I don't want to intrude. I'll have to get back to the station this afternoon."

"Please, you came all the way up here. We're about to have brunch." After all, if Sam hadn't shown up, I don't know if we ever would have seen Ellen's presents. Evidence of crimes tend to stay in lockers forever. Or at least until after trial. He worked hard to get these for us.

"Well, when food is on the line, I can't say no." When he smiles at me, I know he's here for more than the food.

We take our time relishing Ellen's thoughtfulness, and I know these are gifts we will never part with. We laugh, we cry, and Casey and Brax choose that moment to announce they are pregnant. It's truly a Christmas celebration.

Mom puts the food on the table, and we all gather around talking about what we're grateful for. Thad pokes at me about sitting in his seat. We argue lightly about who sat where growing up, and Mom reminds us that none of us had assigned seats. Not to mention, our dinner table has expanded with spouses and will grow again with kids next year.

Yeah, I've decided there will be a next year. What are the holidays without family and traditions? We fill our plates, and Dad taps on a glass. We quiet down and automatically raise ours in reply.

"To living every day as if it's our last," Dad says.

"Dark!" Casey quips with a smile. "To new beginnings."

"To living healthy lives," Thad says with an arm around Melly.

"To remembering fond memories of the past," I say.

"To Ellen," Mom says.

We clink glasses in agreement.

**If you like US Marshals Mak and Wilton, read book 1, *When They Disappeared*, in A Mak and Wilton series.**

## PROLOGUE
MADDOX

Despite the chilly weather outside, the real cold was the stony atmosphere coming from inside the Aston Martin that the Casa Cipriani hotel had provided to the popular star-crossed lovers. When the shiny, black sports car rolled to a stop in front of the Battery Maritime Building located on the edge of the East River, Selah Lablanc flung open the door without hesitation.

She stuck one long shapely leg out of the car, then the other. Her Christian Louboutin black pumps with signature red soles touched the ground. She stood regally for a moment, like a queen assessing her subjects. Her vintage black blazer and pantsuit had been a steal from Saks Fifth Avenue. But her perfectly coordinated handbag was easily worth over twelve thousand dollars. She smiled at the group of fans huddled outside their hotel. She winked and gave them her famous double-hand wave.

Maddox Miller, an NFL football player, who had also been dressed by the best, wore an Armani double-breasted suit custom tailored for his six-foot-four-inch body and fit to accommodate his 220 pounds of lean muscle. A gold hoop earring winked from his ear. Maddox was a little more reluctant to leave the limo, trying not to let his irritation over the public adoration show. As per his agreement with Selah, Maddox made the choice to do what was expected of him. He got out, came around the car, and grabbed Selah's hand, making sure to stand close enough that their shoulders touched.

The crowd went wild.

"Kiss her!" someone shouted.

He laughed in mock surprise and leaned over to gently kiss Selah's signature red lips. He even swept her long blonde hair to the side and put an arm around her shoulders, which he kept there as he broke the kiss. He put his free hand up in mock humility.

"Okay, okay, we've gotta get in there," Maddox said.

Though Selah looked at him with adoration in her eyes and smiled that brilliant, red-lipped smile that used to make his heart somersault, he felt her body tense. He knew he would never hear the end of this one.

He dropped his arm and grabbed her hand again, gently leading her forward, but it felt like they were clinging to each other in more of a death grip. They walked through the crowd, all smiles and waves to the fans.

Once they were in the hotel, they barely noticed the luxurious lobby with its Art Deco features, jazzy music playing in the background, and chic Italian vibe. The ceilings were vaulted and there was a tiled fireplace along the wall. This was the kind of place where Maddox would love to relax and hang out if only they could ditch their trail of paparazzi.

The concierge greeted them crisply, smoothing the front of his Italian suit, and immediately ushered them into a private elevator which took them directly to the Riverview Penthouse Suite.

The room had cashmere wall coverings. Like the lobby, Art Deco fixtures and pictures on the wall adorned the suite with matching Italian tiles. But the view from the private terrace is what sealed the deal for Selah. She adored a good view.

Once they were alone in their hotel room and the door had swung shut, they dropped hands as though the touch had been burning them.

It was supposed to be a private getaway after a special appearance on *The Entertainment Today Show*. One last fling before Selah went on tour and Maddox went to play in the big rivalry game.

"This is over," Maddox declared in a low and strong voice.

"I know. What a relief!" Selah responded, her eyes on the Statue of Liberty, which they could see from their room. She kicked off her Louboutins. "The fans are getting worse, I think. Speaking of which, what in the world were you thinking by talking to them? You know you can't give them too much attention!"

"I don't think you understand what I just said to you. I'm saying this is over. Us. We are over. I'm done." He looked deeply into her eyes, making sure she understood his words.

She froze, standing stock still with wide, surprised eyes and stared at him like she could not comprehend his words. Maddox braced himself for what he knew would come next. Selah liked to get her way and she would do anything to get it. This was not going to go well. But they'd been on the brink of a break-up for a while. She shouldn't be surprised.

"But what will everyone think?" she asked in a whisper, her eyes full of fear.

"That's what you have to say right now?" He shook his head and picked up his phone. He dialed and put the phone up to his ear. "I need an exit out of here. Can you put together a quick plan?" He paused, listening, before he continued. "I'll be leaving separately. We definitely don't want this to leak, so if you could be extra discreet here, that would be great. Thanks!" Maddox hung up the phone.

He turned back to Selah. Her eyes seemed to be swimming with tears. He hesitated for a moment. He'd never seen her cry before. Was he making a mistake?

"Hey," he said softly as he closed the gap between them and put his hand on her shoulder. "You're gonna be just fine."

She wiped her tears with irritation. The moment was gone. She put her shoulders back and stood up taller, her composure firmly back in place. "I have no idea how we're going to spin this one," she snapped bitterly.

He felt his wall go back up and irritation settled back in its normal place. He should've known that all she would care about was her public image. He had fallen for her manipulations so many times to get him to so many events. The truth was, he was tired. He was a football player, so that was saying a lot.

"Can we end this amiably, please?" Maddox asked. Then he ducked to avoid the pillows she began throwing at him. She seemed to throw anything within reach. He was lucky pillows were all she had at her fingertips at the moment.

"Get out!" Selah screamed loudly. "I don't need you. I never did."

"Gladly," he said, feeling resigned. She didn't seem to notice he had not even brought a bag. This had been his plan from the beginning.

He checked his phone as he opened the hotel door. He glanced back and could see Selah's back to him, her shoulders shaking. So, she *was* crying. Maddox felt a wave of sadness wash over him.

On cue, as the door swung shut behind him, his phone started ringing. It was his publicist—a person he'd never needed before he met Selah. She had an escape plan for him. Relief flooded through him as he stepped onto the elevator and out of Selah's life. He realized he was done with the limelight, even if just for the moment. The NFL was different from Hollywood. He had figured that out the hard way.

As the elevator doors closed behind him, he sighed and pushed down his emotions. He wondered if she could have just been her, without all the fame, and if he could have just been him, a successful tight end for Kansas City, would they have actually had a chance to make the relationship work?

He supposed he'd never know the answer to that. He pushed open the door to the back entrance of the hotel. Limo in sight, Maddox stepped into the daylight. He looked around, satisfied that there were no paparazzi peeking over the privacy wall behind the hotel and that the limo was wedged comfortably on a one-way street that would lead to his freedom.

He never saw it coming. He squinted at the bright sun overhead, thinking he must have left his sunglasses somewhere. He nodded to the limo driver, who was standing by the door the driver had opened for Maddox. As Maddox stepped forward to duck into the limo, he felt a slight sting on his neck which he assumed was a sweat bee. He swiped at his neck as he settled himself in the comfortable seat of the luxury car, unaware that sweat bee was really a needle with fluid in it.

The door closed beside him.

Peace settled over him as he sat in that quiet, nondescript limo. The next minute, he was unconscious.

## CHAPTER 1
### WILTON

Stephen Wilton rolled over and put a hand on his girlfriend's bare shoulder, scooted over to it, and then kissed it. He smiled when Kristie mumbled something incoherent. She wasn't a morning person. He was, but he thought he could watch her sleep all day.

Her eyes flickered open. "Are you watching me sleep again?"

"Guilty," he smiled.

Kristie threw the comforter off and sat up in one graceful movement. He could see the swan-like arc of her back and the curve of her firm bottom. Her shapely legs were long and slim. She reached for the clothes she had been wearing last night and began pulling them on.

For a moment, her long, brown hair that waved down

her back reminded him of *her*. Yes, perhaps he had a type. Brown hair, green eyes, stubborn, and independent. Kristie slid her pants on and turned around as she snapped her bra into place. She hesitated.

"Honestly, Stephen." She took three steps back to the bed and laid back down. She rubbed the comforter suggestively. "I could do this with you all day. I mean, look at you. You're easily the hottest guy I've ever met. With your curly blond hair, baby blues, and that body..." She trailed a finger over his six pack.

"But?" he asked, knowing what was coming next. *Love 'Em and Leave 'Em* was his nickname at the office. That's because he always seemed to be dating a different girl. What the people at the office didn't know was that it wasn't Stephen who was doing the leaving.

"*But* I'm not what you're looking for." Kristie picked up a picture off his nightstand. It was a picture of Paige, who was laughing with a younger version of his daughter, Anna.

"That's a picture of my daughter. It was a good memory—"

"Right, a picture of your daughter *and* your baby mama, Paige. Come on, Stephen. Don't you think that's weird? It's like you're advertising that you're still in love with your ex. And by the way, all you want in life is a family. *This* family."

"That's not fair," Stephen protested weakly. Her words stung because they were true.

Kristie shrugged, leaned over, and kissed Stephen. "Like I said, I could do this all day long. You call me if you want a good time. But I'm not the girl you're going to put a ring on."

"Oh no!" Stephen sat up, suddenly horrified. "You found the ring?"

Kristie's long, perfectly manicured fingernails tapped

the nightstand drawer. "You don't keep it very well hidden. Good gosh, Stephen, we've been seeing each other for three months!"

"It's not—it's not what you think," Stephen defended himself.

"Well, either it's for me or it's not—and I'm not sure which is more disturbing—but the fact remains, you have a wedding ring in your nightstand drawer." She got up again and pulled on her shirt.

"It wasn't for you," Stephen said quietly.

"Was it hers?" Kristie pointed to the picture of Paige. She adjusted her shirt, smoothing it against her body.

"No, actually." Stephen got up out of bed and pulled on a pair of boxer briefs. He sat down on the edge of the bed and wondered if he looked as rejected as he felt.

Now Kristie hesitated. "There was a second potential missus? Do tell."

Stephen sighed. It wasn't a story he wanted to relive. It wasn't something he talked about. He'd met Carley Smith a few years ago, long after Paige had ended things with him. They'd lived together and raised Anna for a year before she'd broken up with Stephen. But Carley quickly decided she couldn't live without Anna and kidnapped her while Stephen was away and Anna was with his parents. In an attempt to keep Anna and make the police stop looking for her, Carley faked her and Anna's deaths. Stephen was left in agony that two people he loved in his life were suddenly dead. When he realized they were actually still alive, he'd found and tracked Carley down. Except he had arrived minutes too late. She had been shot in the abdomen and then died in his arms. He found Anna minutes later, unharmed—physically. They found out later that four-year-old Anna had witnessed the murder.

"No?" Kristie replied to Stephen's silence. "That's the thing about you, Stephen. You fall hard for a woman, start planning a wedding, but you don't know how to be vulnerable or open enough to get her down the aisle."

Stephen's phone started ringing. He glanced at the screen. It was the office.

"Then there's that." Kristie pointed to his phone. She slipped on her shoes, walked a few steps to him, and kissed him a long good-bye. "Call me if you need a little fun."

Stephen watched her go, thinking sadly about why he couldn't ever make them stay. Was he really that unlovable?

His phone rang again, and he answered this time.

"Stephen? How fast can you get here? We have a new case." Deputy Director Rob Sikes was all business.

"I can be there in twenty minutes," Stephen said, knowing it would take him five to shower. He hung up. As he quickly showered, turned off the hot water, and toweled off, he thought about Kristie's words.

While his daughter, Anna, was his family, she didn't live with him. He did want to have a full-time family of his own someday. He would love to get married and maybe even have another child or two. But right now, he was married to his job. That would have to be enough.

**Order book 1, *When They Disappeared*, of A Mak and Wilton Thriller series.**

# ALSO BY ADDISON MICHAEL

**A Mynart Mystery Thriller** series is ghostly suspense with psychological elements. If you like complex heroines, paranormal twists and turns, and gripping suspense, then you'll love this dark glimpse into the psyche.

Book 1 - *What Comes Before Dawn*

Book 2 - *Dawn That Brings Death*

Book 3 - *Truth That Dawns*

Book 4 - *Dawn That Breaks*

Book 5 - *What Comes After Dawn*

***The Other AJ Hartford*** - A phantom on a train. A mysterious kidnapping long ago. Can she connect the dots before all her futures disappear forever? If you like good-hearted heroines, ghostly phenomena, and nail-biting high stakes, then you'll love this mind-blowing adventure.

**A Mak and Wilton Thriller** series is a pulse-pounding crime thriller series with a strong female lead, stimulating twists, and relentless suspense.

Book 1 - *When They Disappeared*

Book 2 - *When She Vanished*

Book 3 - *Why He Lied*

Book 4 - *Why She Fled*

Book 5 - *Why He Died*

# REVIEW REQUEST

*If you enjoyed this book, I would be extremely grateful if you would leave a brief review on the store site where you purchased your book or on Goodreads. Your review helps fellow readers know what to expect when they read this book.*

*Thank you in advance!*

*~ Addison Michael*

# ABOUT THE AUTHOR

Addison Michael is the oldest of six siblings. She grew up with a golden reputation and a well-hidden dark side. Writing became her outlet. Addison's dark side emerges in the crime and mystery thrillers she writes today. She lives in the Midwest and believes in writing what she knows, so her stories are often set in the Midwest region. From cabins surrounded by acres of desolate woods to rural police departments and eclectic personalities, Addison Michael captures the essence of small-town living.

You'll find the following tropes in Addison Michael thriller books:

- Cabin in the woods
- You can't go home again...
- Unreliable narrator
- Kidnapping/missing person
- Addiction/recovery
- Femme fatale
- Serial killer

www.ingramcontent.com/pod-product-compliance
Lightning Source LLC
Chambersburg PA
CBHW071552110726
47908CB00007B/2075